# AMBER FISHER

# ONLY SIN DEEP

LIGHTS, CAMERA, MYSTERY

2

# intro reel (recap)

Welcome to *Sinful House*, a reality TV show where the 7 Deadly Sins live together in the sunny beach town of Odyssey, California, and compete to become America's Favorite Sin!

Previously on *Sinful House:*

1.  Pride and Lust were assigned the task of figuring out who was behind the cursed fortune cookies at the Chinese restaurant Wights and Wongs.
2.  Sloth, Gluttony, and Envy won Good Samaritan points for completing their task first. They were tasked with finding Mrs. Romanowsky's missing son…
3.  ….Who turned up dead in an industrial freezer at Wights and Wongs.
4.  Upon investigating, Pride discovered that the dead man, Walt Romanowsky, was a

member of a supernatural bounty hunting organization called Chenoweth International. His mother asked Sloth and Pride to investigate the organization.

5. After breaking into the morgue, Pride laid hands on Walt's corpse and had a vision of the person who killed him. It turned out to be the sous chef from Wights and Wongs, Ping…

6. ….Who was later revealed to be a nine-tailed fox disguised as a human.

7. The network's producer, Tricia Woodward, asked Pride to investigate the missing Sam Lovelace art commune and discover the truth about Sid Sheridan's (aka Pride's) past.

*You're all caught up! Stay tuned for more rollicking adventures. And don't forget to vote for your favorite sin at the end of each challenge.*

*Happy watching!*

# one

. . .

"I don't think that should go there."

Gluttony placed his hands on the brand new foosball table and leaned into his palms. Envy stood akimbo, scowling at the game. Her brows were furrowed, and her mouth twisted as though the table had done something naughty and she was deciding its punishment.

"Then where exactly do you think it should go, Envy?"

Envy hrmmed, thinking as she looked around the space, analyzing potential placements. "I'm not sure, but my intuition says it can't go there."

Currently, the foosball table sat in the center of the room, which made sense since foosball required a lot of space. It couldn't go flush against any of the walls. "If you have a better idea about where to put it," Gluttony said with exaggerated patience, "I'm all ears. But I'm not about to let you tell me that this ain't a good place without you telling me where *is* a good place."

Envy circled the offending foosball table, rubbing her chin with her fingertips as she considered her options. "No, I get it, Gluttony. And I'm not trying to be difficult. But if we're gonna do this, we should do it right. Putting the table there blocks the energy flow between the entry and the doors leading to the patio. That's just bad feng shui. It'll screw up the house energy. Is that what you want? Do you want to live with bad energy?"

Gluttony threw up his hands. "*What* bad energy? Besides the obvious, I mean." He stood tall then, shoulders square, and I realized for the first time how imposing Gluttony could be. I'd always thought of him as a giant teddy bear—which he was—but given his heft and height, he could pull out the intimidation with the best of them.

Envy blinked. "What obvious? Do you feel bad energy? Is there something I should know?"

Gluttony sighed, shaking his head. "I meant we are seven psychopaths living in a house together competing to win a reality show. I'd say any good juju we had coming into this mess has long since fled the coop."

I cleared my throat as I walked into the room, letting the other two know I was there. "We're not psychopaths," I corrected. "Well, I can't speak for Wrath or Greed. But the rest of us are not psychopaths. Psychologically damaged, sure. Mentally—"

"Were you even invited to this conversation?" Gluttony asked.

I hesitated, eyes darting between my housemates. "Not that I'm aware of," I stammered.

"Then you best see your way out of it. Unless you know where this table should go."

"I'm just saying you shouldn't say glib things like calling the other housemates psychopaths." I gestured discreetly toward the room's always-on camera. "We don't want to give people the wrong impression."

"Either way," Gluttony continued, returning his attention to Envy, "there isn't a better place to put the foosball table. I don't know anything about feng shui, but this is the only place big enough. So unless we put it on the patio—"

"It can't go on the patio," I interjected. "If it rains, it'll get destroyed. Plus, the heat will probably warp it, and the humidity will definitely rust it." I had no idea if that was true, but it sounded plausible.

"I know it can't go outside," Gluttony grumbled, running his hands over his afro. "I was being facetious. Do you know what that means? Facetious?"

I glowered at him. "I'm not an idiot."

"Then quit acting like it!" Gluttony cursed under his breath, then pointed a finger at Envy. "You know what? You don't like where I put the table, put it wherever you want. I'm gonna go make breakfast."

We watched as Gluttony stalked out of the room. After a moment, Envy's shoulders slumped, and she let out her breath in a whoosh. "Well, if there wasn't negative energy in here before, there is now." She hugged her torso and made puppy dog eyes at me. "I was just trying to be helpful. In a house this size with this many people, protecting our energy is really important. You'd think Gluttony would understand that."

I cocked an eyebrow. "Why would Gluttony understand that?"

"He's a kitchen witch," she said, as though this were the most obvious thing in the world. "Witches work with energy, don't they? I think I read that somewhere."

I shrugged. "Maybe, but I don't get the feeling Gluttony is that kind of witch. Outside of food, magic doesn't seem to be his bag."

Envy didn't respond to that, but I saw the way her nose wrinkled and her ears perked up, like she sensed something was amiss. "Yeah, I can feel it. Negative energy all over the place. It's too bad our housekeepers can't do spiritual cleanses. Maybe I'll just…"

Before Envy finished her thought, a breeze fluttered through my hair, raising goosebumps on my skin. The faint smell of incense filled my nose. Across the room, a diaphanous creature composed of smoke materialized before the large glass doors overlooking the beach. She shimmered into view like a mirage. She had long, slender limbs like a human's, except she had no hands or feet. Her limbs merely faded into nothingness. The creature moved gracefully, wafting around the room and moving her arms in choreographed patterns. She looked like she was dancing. Or perhaps casting a spell.

I watched the elemental for a moment before I turned to Envy. "Did you do that?" I lifted my chin in the creature's direction.

Envy, too, was watching the creature with rapt attention. "I guess so," she said. "Not consciously. But sometimes, the sylph appears when the energy around me needs cleansing. Look at her! She's trying to purify this space." A soft smile played over her lips as she whispered, "Good girl! You clear out mean old Gluttony's bad juju."

I watched the sylph float around the room, its graceful movements mesmerizing. The air elemental appeared to change colors like a chameleon, the hues of its smoke shifting to match its surroundings. I'd never seen a creature composed of smoke before, so part of me was enthralled. But the rest of me was apprehensive.

"Don't take this the wrong way," I said, "but do you actually have control of this thing? We're not gonna end up in a situation like last time, are we?"

Envy's cheeks glowed pink as she recalled the previous summoning. In a kind-hearted attempt to keep the house clean, Envy accidentally summoned a water elemental and immediately lost control of it. Left to its own devices, the undine had sequestered itself in Sloth's room, where it drenched everything she owned in water. It was a disaster. Half of Sloth's belongings were ruined.

Envy leaned her head to the side, her eyes trailing the sylph's movements around the room. "Control of the sylph? I wonder if such a thing is even possible. They do what they like. But don't worry!" She must have sensed my growing unease because she laughed and patted me on the shoulder. It was supposed to be reassuring. "Unlike the water elemental, the sylph is harmless! What could possibly go wrong?"

I groaned, clasping my hands on top of my head. "Envy, why did you *say* that? Everyone knows you're never supposed to say that. The minute someone says nothing can go wrong, *something goes catastrophically wrong.* Geez, they made a whole movie about that!"

Envy looked surprised. "They did?"

"Yes!"

"Which movie?"

I held out my hands, exasperated. "*The Titanic!*"

Envy snorted, running a hand through her hair. "Good grief, Pride, that's not what that movie's about. But okay, I take your point. Sylph," she called out, "don't mess anything up, okay? I don't need to be in hot water with America's Favorite Sin."

I made a disapproving sound in my throat and waved away the hyperbole. "Don't call me that," I said. "I haven't earned it. I had one good episode, that's it. I would hardly call that a victory."

We had been living at Sinful House for almost a month, our everyday lives filmed as we adjusted to living with six strangers in the cozy beach town of Odyssey, California. We were the stars of a new reality TV show, competing to become America's Favorite Sin. So far, I was a fan favorite. But the show was still in its infancy. I had plenty of time left to lose.

"The camera loves you," Envy crooned as the two of us walked over to the couch, settling in. "You never can tell who's gonna look good on camera. I thought Lust would be the one to beat. Who would've known it would be you?"

I didn't think Envy intended that to be a slight, so I tried not to take it that way. However, she was right about one thing: I, too, expected Lust to have a better showing than she did. In any case, although the show premiered to record-breaking numbers, there was still a lot of road to travel before any of us would be crowned America's Favorite Sin. The lucky winner would take home an epic prize: their heart's ultimate desire.

"Speaking of being America's Favorite Sin," Envy said, "you're paired up with Wrath for this challenge, right? What's your task?"

"Some rich lady is worried that her sister is being catfished," I said. "Wrath and I are supposed to find out the truth behind her online love interest. Real deal or a shark in sheep's clothing?"

Envy chuckled. "Not a bad challenge, really. Better than the fortune cookie thing, at least. I'm surprised they didn't give you a case with a more supernatural element, though. You know, since you can see ghosts and everything? Especially since you worked the wight case, it seemed like magic and mayhem would be right up your alley. But maybe there's not much paranormal activity in this town aside from us."

"Well, you'll be glad to hear our case does have a paranormal aspect to it. You ready for this?" I stretched the moment out, enjoying torturing my housemate more than a little. From the corner of my eye, I saw the sylph continuing its journey around the room, the smell of incense thickening in my nose. I hoped she was almost done with her cleansing. My allergies were getting to me. "The online boyfriend claims to be the spirit of this woman's dead husband trapped in a medium's body."

For a moment, Envy didn't move. She didn't even blink. Then, as her shock wore off, she burst into laughter. She covered her mouth with her hands, her eyes wide above her fingertips. "You've got to be kidding me! The ghost of her dead husband trapped in a medium's body? And this woman fell for it?"

I shrugged. "I can't say for sure if she fell for it. Wrath and I haven't started investigating, so we haven't even spoken to her. But that's the challenge. So if that is the gist of it…" I shook my head, running a hand through my hair. "They say there's a sucker born every minute. In my experience, the more money a person has, the more likely they are to be a mark."

"Well, I guess that's true," Envy said. "Still, even if it meant everyone would target me, I sure wouldn't mind having all that money. *Or* fame. Can you imagine what it must be like to see yourself in every magazine or be invited to every talk show? To be adored by fans all over the world? Oh, I wouldn't mind that at all. I feel *destined* for stardom. I just *know* it." Her eyes fluttered closed as she smiled dreamily, no doubt imagining herself surrounded by sycophants snapping her photo.

I frowned. "Fame and celebrity aren't what they're cracked up to be. Believe me. I know."

Envy's eyes grew wider. "Oh, you mean because of the missing Sam Lovelace colony thing?"

I nodded. "An entire colony vanished off the face of the Earth, except for me, the baby left behind. People always want to hear my story. I can't tell you how many pitches I've heard for documentaries, books, movies… Even our network told me I need to be investigating my past for this show. They say the viewers are wild for it or something. It's annoying."

Envy nodded, absently tapping a finger to her lips. "Well, what *do* you think happened to them?"

I rolled my eyes. "Not you, too. Look, I don't know. Whether they stepped into another dimension or were abducted by aliens is anyone's guess."

And plenty of people *had* guessed. But I never saw the point in navel-gazing about the past. Besides, it seemed disrespectful. I was raised by two kind people who loved me very much. And despite never feeling very connected to them, they had done their best to make me into a respectable human being.

It wasn't their fault I was nowhere near respectable. Heck, some days, I wasn't even sure I was human.

"Anyway, you wanna help me find a new spot for the foosball table? I think if we move some of the furniture around, we can make it work."

My desire to do physical labor in the interest of improved feng shui was very low, so I checked my watch and made a disappointed face. "Can't. Wrath and I are meeting our client soon." I stood up and gave the sylph a quick parting glance. Turning to Envy, I said, "Keep an eye on that thing, will you?"

My housemate rolled her eyes as she climbed to her feet. "You're overreacting. She's not causing any trouble. By the time dinner rolls around, the energy in this place is gonna be spic and span. You just wait."

I had time for a quick shower before pounding on Wrath's door. He flung it open and flashed me the brightest smile I'd ever seen him wear. "You ready to rock and roll, man?" he asked.

"We're meeting Bailey Preston in fifteen minutes," I said. "Whether I'm ready or not, it's time to go."

We tumbled out the door with a cameraman on our heels. As we pulled out the driveway, I noticed faint tendrils of smoke seeping from the rec room windows.

# two

. . .

"You gotta be kidding me! Is this really it? This is the place?"

As we pulled up to Bailey Preston's mansion, I understood why Wrath was about to have a conniption fit. Don't get me wrong, beautiful homes were in no short supply in Odyssey. But even by Odyssey standards, the Preston mansion was incredible.

We'd already driven down a long private road to get to the house. Now that we were here, it seemed we were in a secret oasis. Palm trees surrounded us, providing welcome shade from an unrelenting sun. The lawn was emerald green and immaculately tended. Precisely sculpted topiaries featuring an array of tropical birds lined the walkway leading to the home's front entry, marked by an enormous stone fountain.

"Pretty impressive," I said to Wrath as the cameraman followed us up to the door. "I've never seen anything like this."

Wrath spun on his heel, his brow creased, eyes cut in

narrow slits. "Impressive? Really? That's what you see? Something beautiful and luxurious?"

I shrugged, digging my hands into my pockets. "Sure. Isn't that what you see?"

Wrath was quiet a moment, his lips pressed into a thin line. Then he said, "How much do you think this house is worth?"

I scratched my chin, dredging up memories of the beautiful buildings I'd seen in Portia Cameron's real estate office. It was the only thing I had for comparison. "I don't know, $10 million? $20 million?"

"$20 million is probably undervaluing it," Wrath said. "I'd put this place closer to $30 million. You see where I'm going with this?"

I considered the question carefully before answering. "Not really," I admitted.

"Where you see beauty and luxury, all I see is excess, selfishness, and the blood, sweat, and tears of the people who paid dearly so that one woman could own a home like this."

"I guess I never thought of it that way," I said, reaching for the doorbell. While I understood Wrath's point, we weren't here to discuss the ethics of extreme wealth. We had a job to do, and the sooner we got started, the sooner we could go back to Sinful House and enjoy some of Gluttony's amazing food. Plus, it was just easier to agree with Wrath. It kept his diatribes to a minimum.

"I see the oppression of the working class," Wrath continued, hands balled into fists at his sides. My finger paused just before hitting the doorbell. "I see people exploited for their labor. I see hungry families, sick children, and parents working two, three jobs just to make ends meet. This isn't beautiful," Wrath said, throwing the house a grievous look. "This is disgusting."

I said nothing as my finger punched the doorbell.

The door opened. Standing in the doorway was a petite woman with sun-streaked blonde hair. She wore a pair of loose-fitting white linen slacks, bejeweled sandals, and an off-the-shoulder yellow peasant blouse. She held a tiny dog in her arms. It was one of those purse dogs, those awful things that yip and yap and snarl, having no idea they were as threatening as the Easter Bunny. I hated those stupid dogs. But this woman's dog didn't bark. It merely looked up at us with wide, shining eyes, its tongue lolling from the side of its mouth.

I hated this particular dog a little less.

"You must be Pride and Wrath," the woman said, a smile spreading over her face. "I'm so glad you could make it! Please, come in."

We stepped inside and were greeted with piano music drifting in from another room. I couldn't tell if it was live music or a recording. In this house, both seemed equally likely. "I'm sorry, where are my manners?" The woman pressed the dog into the crook of her arm and extended a hand. "I'm Bailey Preston. Welcome to my home."

Wrath took her hand first. "Nice to meet you, Bailey. I'm Wrath." He clapped me on the shoulder. "And this is my buddy, Pride." He glanced around him, taking in the ostentation of our surroundings. As I watched his face, my heart skipped a beat, my breath lodged in my throat. The last thing we needed was for Wrath to utter even a fraction of his anti-capitalism screed in front of Bailey. But before I could say anything, his expression changed, a lightning-bright smile breaking out over his face as he gave an appreciative whistle. "Man, this place is off the charts. I've never seen anything like it."

Bailey looked around the entrance hall as though seeing her home for the first time. "Thanks. I can't take credit for any of it, though. My interior designer is an angel. Anyway, I poured drinks for us in the sitting room. Please, follow me."

As Bailey moved down the hallway with her dog tucked under her arm, I got a better look at the place. Disgusting display of obscene wealth aside, the house was terrific. The hallway we were moving down was lined with life-size black-and-white portraits of a man whose style reminded me of Elvis Costello. Alongside these portraits were framed platinum albums. At least two dozen accompanied our trek down the hallway.

"The albums," I said. "Are they yours? Are you a singer?"

Bailey Preston turned around, her eyes wide as saucers. My heart lurched into my throat, and I worried that I'd stepped in it once again. I'm not exactly what you might call a pop culture connoisseur. So if Bailey Preston expected me to recognize her face from a magazine or even a commercial, I wasn't the right person for that. Still, I didn't like to look like a fool, either. I stopped in my tracks, chewing the insides of my cheeks.

But Bailey's bewilderment quickly faded to laughter. "Me? A singer? Oh my goodness, no. Unfortunately, I don't have a musical bone in my body. No, these records belonged to my father. Perhaps you recognize his name? Adam Preston?"

I opened my mouth to say I knew the name—I didn't, but neither she nor the rest of America needed to know that—but Wrath beat me to the punch. "Of *course* we know Adam Preston. He was only the biggest music producer of our time. A mogul. A phenomenon."

"Daddy was unique, that's for sure," Bailey agreed. "When he died, I inherited most of his paraphernalia. Tammy didn't want any of it. I don't know why. But then again, I guess no one really understands Tammy."

We had arrived in the sitting room, which was much more comfortable than I expected based on the furnishings in the other rooms we'd passed by. Instead of chandeliers and Queen Victoria-style fainting couches, the sitting room was decidedly normal. A jumbo-size TV hung over a gas fireplace. An oversized leather couch took up the center of the room, and completing the U shape of the seating area were two smaller love seats. I could see an expanse of beachfront from the enormous windows that composed most of the wall opposite where I stood. The coffee table was set with liquor bottles, club soda, and a silver tray with finger sandwiches.

Wrath and I sat on the couch, and Bailey sat on the loveseat beside us. Her dog curled up in her lap. She pointed to the drinks on the table. "I hope you don't mind what I selected for us. Gin and tonic is my go-to," she said with a grin. "If there's something else you prefer, just let me know. I'll have Baxter bring it in."

Wrath raised an eyebrow. "Baxter?"

Bailey smiled. "One of my personal assistants. When you run a house this size," she gestured around her vaguely, "it's more than a full-time job. And with everything else I have going on, I need all the help I can get. So!" She clapped her hands at her chest, an obvious change in subject. "The two of you are here to talk about the case, right?"

I nodded. "We got the assignments yesterday," I explained. "The email from the network was pretty light on details. Want us to read what they sent?"

Bailey nodded and settled back into the pillows. "Sure, that would be great."

Wrath pulled out his phone. "Show me the Bailey Preston assignment," he said to the device.

His phone flickered to life, taking him immediately to an email from the network presenting the details of our case. Wrath was a technopath—he could get technology to do just about anything he wanted. It was a pretty helpful skill if you asked me. Too bad the guy wielding it was, well, Wrath.

Wrath read aloud. "Heiress Bailey Preston is concerned that her sister, Tamora, is being hoodwinked. For the past six months, Tamora has been talking to a man online who claims he loves her and wants to marry her. However, the two have never met, or even video chatted. Help Bailey find out if Tamora's lover is who he says he is or if he's got other ulterior motives."

Bailey looked down into her lap, but I saw color climbing up her cheeks. "They included something else, right?"

Wrath cleared his throat and read, "The challenge

isn't as simple as it seems. The catch? Tamora's online lover claims to be the spirit of her dead husband trapped in a medium's body."

Bailey looked up, and her face aged before my eyes. For a moment, she was no longer a vibrant socialite with a dumb purse dog. She had a haunted look in her eyes, a darkness that pulled her lips into a frown. "That's the gist of it," she said. "I guess I better start at the beginning."

Bailey leaned forward and selected a tumbler from the coffee table. She filled it with ice before adding the gin and tonic. "Tammy is my older sister. Don't let that fool you. We're about as different as night and day. And although we've always gotten along, we've never been close, if you know what I mean. Still, she's my sister. I look out for her. Because to be honest, she's not very good at looking out for herself."

"What do you mean by that?" Wrath asked.

Bailey took a sip. "She's gullible. She doesn't trust her brain. She relies on gut instinct and 'spiritual advisement,'" Bailey made finger quotes around the phrase, "to make even the most basic life decisions. She's kind of the perfect mark for a scam like this." She stroked the dog in her lap absently, her head listing to one side as she conjured up a memory. "Tammy's husband was Jeff Bishop. Really nice guy. Everybody liked him. And he adored Tammy. I mean, just head over heels in love with her. His family was like ours—big in the music industry. His father was Kerry Bishop, the big-time producer, and his grandfather was Berry Bishop—founder of Bishop Knight Records. Anyway, he and Tammy were married for over five years. And then he had the accident."

Again, she sipped from her drink. Wrath, too, reached for his glass. I left mine untouched. I'm not a teetotaler or anything. But I hadn't even had breakfast yet.

"He trained for years to climb Mount Everest. It was his driving passion—his *raison d'être*. But I guess no matter how hard you prepare or how badly you want something, some people just aren't meant to climb Mount Everest. You know what I mean? So he died up there, just like so many others. Tammy was devastated. She was in mourning so deep, I thought she might never come out. She wouldn't even get out of bed most days."

Bailey heaved a heavy sigh, her shoulders pressed low as she shook her head at the memory. "I was the one who recommended she try online dating. I should've known better. But she was so adamant that she didn't want to date anyone from our circle. She wanted someone normal, someone who knew what it meant to struggle. Jeff was a philanthropist. She wanted someone Jeff would have approved of. A project."

Wrath leaned forward expectantly. "And did she find someone like that?"

Bailey pinched her lips together, her nostrils flaring. "Well, she found *someone*. Leave it to my sister to find the biggest charlatan the Internet has to offer." Bailey lifted the dog from her lap and put him on the ground. She got to her feet and began pacing, arms wrapped around her torso as her fingertips tapped her elbows nervously. "She met this guy online. And at first, it seemed good for her. She was getting back to her old self. But over time, she started acting strange. Tammy's always been strange," she amended, "but... I don't know how to describe it. She got worse. I finally got her drunk one night, and she told me she was seeing this online guy she'd never met, and he wanted to marry her. And the crazier part was, she was considering it. Strongly considering it. Like, she wanted to go wedding dress shopping and everything."

I found all of this fascinating, but maybe not for the reasons other people might be drawn into the story. The part I didn't understand was the *dating* part, let alone online dating. I never dated. Not really. The idea of auditioning to be someone's lover made me want to shrivel up and die. I'm not kidding. I would rather walk into the surf and let my body turn to sea foam like in *The Little Mermaid* before I'd consider *dating*.

(I'm talking about the Hans Christian Andersen original. Not whatever cockamamie nonsense I watched as a kid. In real life, little mermaids rarely get their happy endings. Not that fairytales are real life, but life is hard is what I'm saying.)

"When did your sister reveal, you know. The catch."

Bailey was staring out the window, her back to Wrath and me. I couldn't see her face or read her expression—not that I was very good at that anyway—but I heard the weariness in her voice when she said, "Three or four weeks ago. She said she was determined to make the relationship work because the online mystery man was Jeff. Just... Jeff trapped in someone else's body."

"And how does *that* work?" I asked.

Bailey turned around slowly, refusing to meet my eyes. "You'll have to ask my sister. I didn't ask for the details because I don't care. There's no such thing as an afterlife. There's certainly no such thing as ghosts. When Jeff died, he just died. No piece of him lingered around. No energy got left behind. Jeff's just gone. Like my dad and my mom. Like everyone else who has ever died and will ever die. So this idea about him being trapped anywhere, let alone in someone else's body? It's hocus-pocus nonsense. And I need my sister to understand that. I need her to get her act together and gather the pieces of her life before it's too late."

I cleared my throat and cracked my fingers. "Well, sure, but you're wrong about the ghosts, though. They're absolutely real."

When Bailey turned a dubious look in my direction, Wrath scooted forward, placing a hand on my knee. "What Pride means is people believe in that stuff. So we have to take it seriously."

I stared at Wrath. "That's not what I meant. I meant exactly—"

"Anyway," Wrath interrupted, shooting me a dark glare, "it doesn't matter about the ghosts. Even if Jeff was trapped in some other dude's body, that wouldn't make him a ghost, right? Ghosts are a dead end." He said this last part more to me than Bailey. "No pun intended."

I returned Wrath's glare but said nothing. Pun or no, Wrath was dead wrong. Ghosts were real. I saw them all the time and had been seeing them since I was a kid.

Mostly, they left me alone. Once in a while, they asked for help. Sometimes they wanted to contact a loved one. Occasionally, they wanted revenge. Most of the time, they just wanted to talk to someone about why they hadn't crossed over. But like Bailey, I didn't know anything about the afterlife. I had no idea if spirits could travel back and forth. The paranormal left many mysteries unsolved, but I knew one thing for sure. Life—and death—were both stranger than most people gave them credit for.

Which isn't to say that the deceased Jeff Bishop was trapped in someone else's body. Even a ghost whisperer like me could be skeptical of a claim like that.

"Anyway, that's why I contacted the network. I knew the police couldn't help. He hasn't asked my sister for money or anything like that. So I can't even press charges— not that I would know what charges to press. But I need someone to help with this. I'm so afraid that this person is taking advantage of my sister. She's already emotionally fragile. The last thing I need is for her to be financially fleeced as well. So can you help? Do you think you can discover who's been pretending to be my sister's dead husband?"

"We're for sure gonna try," Wrath said, once again turning on a charm I had never seen him display before. "Don't you worry, Bailey. Pride and I are on the case. We're gonna win this thing." He blinked and started, shaking himself. "Uh, I mean, we're gonna solve this thing. It's all gonna work out. You'll see."

It was in that fleeting moment that I finally under-stood. All Wrath's fake charm? It wasn't about helping

Bailey. It was about the viewers. Of course it was. How could I have missed it earlier? The real Wrath was a short-tempered, foul-mouthed pain in the neck, just like I thought. This new person was a caricature. A figment of the audience's imagination.

To be honest, I wasn't sure if I was revolted or impressed. It was probably a useful talent to have. The ability to adopt an entirely new personality, I mean. If I could do that, I might try it. The personality I was born with wasn't working out so hot, after all.

# three

. . .

When we arrived back at Sinful House, it was on fire.

Wrath stared at the house, eyes wide with shock. "What the…?"

I swore, fumbling to unbuckle my seatbelt. "You've got to be kidding me." When I got it unlatched, I threw my door open.

Wrath and I jumped from the car, running pell-mell toward the house. I threw open the front door and immediately began coughing. Enormous clouds of billowing smoke poured out of the entryway, stinging my eyes and the back of my throat.

It wasn't just any regular smoke, however. It smelled alarmingly like patchouli.

I darted into the house. "Envy! Sloth! Is anybody here?"

Outside, I heard the scream of sirens as fire trucks pulled up to the property. The smoke was so dense, I could scarcely see, but I wasn't about to let my housemates be asphyxiated. I buried my nose in the crook of my arm as I searched the house for anyone passed out on the floor. I made it all the way upstairs before I heard someone shouting my name.

"Pride? Outside! We're all outside!"

I dashed back down the stairs and was almost at the front door when I saw her—that stupid sylph Envy summoned to cleanse the house. She was still drifting from room to room, tendrils of herbal smoke trailing in her wake.

I growled. When things settled down, Envy and I were gonna need to have a serious talk.

I raced out the door to find firefighters lugging hoses from the truck. I waved my arms overhead, trying to get their attention, but to no avail. They were doing firemen things, shouting to each other and going into the house looking for the fire.

Little did they know, there was no fire to locate. Just a nuisance of a sylph wreaking billowing, herbal havoc.

When I could finally breathe again, I found Envy sitting on the curb, her head cradled in her arms, shoulders shaking. I sat down next to her, but not too close. She, too, reeked of patchouli. "The sylph?" I asked.

Envy didn't raise her head. "I don't understand why this is happening," she said. "I've had problems with the elementals before, sure, but never anything like this. It's like the more I try to help out, the more determined they are to destroy everything!" She sat up now, her face turned toward me. She wasn't exactly crying, but she didn't exactly look thrilled, either. If I had to guess, I'd say she looked scared.

Well, if I were in her position, I'd be scared, too. Scared of Wrath screaming at me. Scared of Gluttony giving me the cold shoulder. Scared of the other housemates being furious all their belongings would smell like hippies for a long, long time.

"I think one of the neighbors called the fire department."

I looked up to find Lust ambling toward us, her hands dug in her back hip pockets. "We were on the other side of town, and even we heard the sirens. I don't think anybody was home once the smoke started getting bad. Everybody wants to win so much, we all got an early start on the day. Even Sloth was actually out of the house before the morning was over."

I stood and dusted myself off, turning my attention back to the house. I noticed now that all the windows were open, smoke billowing out like from a dragon's nostrils. If I had to guess—I was doing a lot of guessing today, apparently—Envy had done that. She was trying to air the place out. It might've worked if she'd been able to reel in the sylph. But that thing was still inside, making more smoke.

I would have liked to see the firemen's faces when they saw what they were up against.

"I guess we're going out to lunch," I said, trying to change the subject. "It's not like we can cook with the house like this. Anybody have any suggestions? I'm starving."

Behind me, I heard Envy sniffle. "I'm not hungry."

"I could go for some seafood," Lust said. "Should I get the group together?"

As contestants on the show, our contracts required us to spend time together as a household. Of course, investigating our cases and solving mysteries for the locals was our top priority. But the second priority was camaraderie. And by camaraderie, I actually mean drama. You just can't have a good reality TV show without a healthy dose of drama. Forcing us to get together for meals was one way the network hoped to stir up theatrics.

"Sure, get a group together," I said. "Looks like we're all gonna need the distraction. So." I cleared my throat and rubbed my hands together, feeling the heat rising in my cheeks. Talking to Lust always turned me into a stammering idiot. "How did your morning go?"

Lust flipped her hair over her shoulder and shrugged. "Fine, I guess. It's weird not to be working with you, though. Your instincts are so much better than everyone else's."

I felt the color in my cheeks deepen at this small compliment. Of course I was better than the other housemates at investigation. After all, that's what I used to do for a living. Before I got fired, I worked with the San Diego Police Department on cases with a paranormal bent. My most recent claim to fame was finding the key witness in a high-profile murder case. There'd been a ghost in the parking garage who had seen everything. I found the spirit, interviewed him, and found the key evidence against the prime suspect. That guy was going away for a long time, thanks to me.

Of course, my skills being second-to-none didn't

matter in the end. Budget cuts, you see. The almighty dollar always wins out.

"Everybody will get better at their jobs as time goes on," I said. I wasn't sure I believe that, but it was likely. Possible. At least plausible. "What is your case, anyway?"

Lust sighed, her nose wrinkled. "Helping some old guy locate his missing antique guns."

"The police weren't interested in the case?"

Lust shrugged. "Apparently, the Odyssey Police are too busy investigating suspicious deaths. I guess this town has a super high death rate?"

I nodded, looking down at my hands. "That would explain why you and I saw so many corpses in the morgue. Well, holler if you need me." I cringed as soon as the words were out of my mouth. I wasn't a "holler if you need me" sort of person, but sometimes Lust made me say and do things out of character.

"Of course I need you," she said, her voice so low, I almost missed it.

I turned, blinking in surprise. But she was already going the other way, heading over to gather the others.

My face caught fire, and my heart skipped. As much as I hated to admit it, I was grinning like a moron.

Lust said she needed me.

Sinful House might be coughing out ungodly amounts of patchouli smoke, but my day was looking up.

———

Later that night, long after the fire department left and the house had aired out enough for human habitation, it was time to visit Tamora Preston—our possible catfishee.

Tamora lived only a few blocks away from Bailey, but her home was much less ostentatious than her sister's. That was a relief because I wasn't sure I could take another of Wrath's rants about the capitalist agenda. We rang the doorbell, and a moment later, the door creaked open.

The woman standing in the doorway looked nothing like I expected. Unlike Bailey, who was petite and tan and blonde, this woman was tall and milk pale with hair as black as a raven's wing. Her hair was cut in a severe bob that ended just beneath her ears. Her bangs were cut into a sharp triangle, the point of which sat directly between two perfectly arched black brows. She was wearing something black and flimsy and silky that looked more like lingerie than a dress. She'd paired the slip with a pair of clunky black combat boots with a 2-inch platform. A silver pentagram hung around her neck. Her lips were painted black, and heavily lined eyes squinted at us in the darkness.

I was so stricken by her appearance that I just stood there, staring. Thankfully, Wrath found his voice easily. "Uh, hey. Are you Tammy Preston?"

The woman in the doorway gave Wrath a long, slow blink. Her face was a mask of ice and venom when she said, "Call me Tammy again, and those will be the last words you ever speak."

I didn't mean to smile, but I did. I understood that

sentiment. I didn't respond well to people calling me Sidney, either. I preferred Sid. Names are important.

"Sorry. Tamora," Wrath supplied. "My name's Wrath. We're here with —"

Tamora held up a hand, interrupting the introduction. "I know who you are," she said, eyes flickering toward the cameras behind us. "You're the idiots from that show. My sister sent you. She said you were coming."

Wrath nodded. "Yeah, that's right. Is it cool if we come in?"

Tamora looked us up and down, sizing us up. I wasn't sure how we rated. I was dressed in a casual t-shirt and jeans, but Wrath looked like something out of a cyberpunk movie. He had taken extra time with his bleached-blond hair today, spiking it out all over his head. He wore a pair of skinny black pants with entirely too many pockets pushed up to his calves. A spiked leather belt at his waist dripped with silver chains, and his wrists sported matching black sweatbands. He also wore combat boots, but he'd left them unlaced, their tongues hanging out. A cropped black hoodie completed the outfit, even though it was almost 80 degrees out.

The door creaked as Tamora swung it open and led us through the living room. The overall effect of the place was something like a baroque nightmare. Every flat surface was covered with black candles, taxidermy ravens, and statues of nude goddesses. The walls were adorned with paintings derived from Tarot cards, each depicting the darker scenes: Death, the Tower, the Devil.

Along one wall, Tamora had created a shrine to her

late husband. Photographs of Jeff Bishop interspersed with candles and various gemstones cluttered an altar. There were photos from their wedding, photos of Jeff as a child, even hand-drawn portraits of him. He'd been a good-looking man. In the photos of them together, they looked very much in love. Not that you can't fake that sort of thing, but.

Wrath nudged me in the side. "Do you have holy water on you?" he whispered. "I think we might need it."

Tamora called over her shoulder, "I heard that."

We continued through the dark, overly air-conditioned house to climb a set of winding stairs. When we reached the landing, Wrath sidled up to our host, pushing up the sleeves on his hoodie. "Thanks for having us. Do you think we could get some water or something? I'm parched. We had a fire at our house, and the smoke did a number on my throat," he explained.

She answered without turning around. "I heard it wasn't a fire. I heard one of the other idiots who lives with you summoned an air elemental she couldn't control and filled the whole place with incense."

Wrath looked at me, and I shrugged. News travels fast in small towns.

"Yeah. Envy's not an idiot, though. I mean, she's okay. So anyway, about that water…"

The woman turned to Wrath and brought a finger to her lips. "I'll get you anything you want, but it'll have to wait. Right now, we have other business to attend to."

"Other business?"

Saying nothing more, the woman pushed open a door and led us into an enormous library. In the center of the room was a rectangular table covered with flickering black candles. That explained the air conditioner, then. Candles put out more heat than you think.

The candles were nestled among pink and red rose petals strewn across the table. A cone of incense burned on a censer shaped like a pentacle to match the star Tamora wore at her throat. Framed photographs were lined up in the center, and seated around the table were six other people who all looked up as we entered the room.

There were three empty chairs.

Tamora swept her arm in front of her. "Take your seats," she said to us. "It doesn't matter where. Any empty seat is fine."

I hesitated, hands clenched at my sides. I don't do well in new situations, and I definitely had no idea what was happening here. Who were these people? What was going on? We were supposed to be interviewing Tamora, not participating in…whatever this was.

Oh God, was this an intervention?

I was deciding whether to turn around and get out of there when Wrath pulled out the nearest chair and slid into place.

Tamora lifted her eyes to me. I was still standing, rooted to the spot. A smile cracked over her lips, but it wasn't exactly friendly. She looked more like a snake about to strike. "We can't get started until you sit down," she said.

What choice did I have? I sat down.

Tamora chose the last seat and folded her hands on the table, smiling for real now. "Thank you all for coming," she said. "And special thanks to you, Madam Andromeda. We are so honored that you broke your vow of seclusion to be with us today."

Now I snapped to attention. Before that moment, I hadn't looked at the faces of the other guests. I don't exactly suffer from face blindness. It's just that my interest in other people is pretty low. But now, I looked. I recognized one of these people. Seated at the head of the table was someone whose persona I knew well.

Andromeda Clark was the premier psychic medium in the country, if not the world. She had appeared on countless talk shows, and for a while, even had a show of her own. I was addicted to her show—I watched every episode, and not just because we shared a professional interest in spirits.

It was because she was captivating.

A few years ago, she canceled her show and went into seclusion, withdrawing from the world to pursue what she called "communion with her holy guardian angel," whatever that meant.

And yet, here she was.

Which meant this wasn't just some weird gathering of friends.

This was a séance.

"Please, just call me Andromeda." The woman grinned, a cupid's smile if I ever saw one. Long, curly pink hair fell over her shoulders. She was wearing something transparent and silvery that could have been the dressing gown to the lingerie Tamora wore. Still, it worked for her. Andromeda had always had an other-worldly style.

"I assume this is everyone, then?" Andromeda asked, turning her attention to our host.

Tamora nodded. "We're ready to begin."

Andromeda cleared her throat and sat forward, placing both palms flat on the table. She looked around the room and slowed her breathing, her eyelids growing heavy. "As most of you know, this world is not conclusion. Beyond what the average person can see, hear, smell, touch, or taste is another realm just as rich and abundant as this one. It is separated from us not by fact but by fiction. We have been conditioned not to believe, but our belief is not required. The other world stands between and among us, and sometimes within us." She dipped her chin toward her chest, her voice growing deeper and more mysterious. "At your invitation, tonight I will endeavor to channel your friends and family from the other side. Do I have any requests?"

I looked around the table and saw that everyone else was doing the same thing. Most everyone looked sheepish, hesitant to speak up. Finally, an older man sitting directly across from me raised a hand. "I have a request," he said. "I'd like to speak to my mother."

Andromeda smiled, tossing a stray curl from her face. "It's always the mothers," she teased. The man blushed, but Andromeda tutted, her smile growing. "I'm only kidding. And your mother's name?"

"Caitlin Pratchett," he said.

"And is Ms. Pratchett's photograph among those on the table?"

The man nodded and selected the photo nearest him, passing it down the table. "That's her," he said.

Andromeda took the photograph and gazed at it before replacing it on the table with a crisp nod. "She was a beautiful woman. I usually like to have an item from the deceased," she said. "Did you bring anything personal of your mother's? Perhaps a piece of jewelry or a special item of clothing?"

The man reached into his smoking jacket's breast pocket and pulled out a glittering tennis bracelet. This, too, he passed down the table. "My father gave this to her on their 50th anniversary," he said. "She should have been buried in it. But my sister…" The man's lips pulled into a frown. "Well. You know how catty some people can be when money is involved."

Andromeda said nothing as she fingered the diamonds, clenching the bracelet in her palm and closing her eyes. A moment later, she breathed out a low, controlled breath and placed the jewelry on the table. Her eyes fluttered open. "Let us begin. Please, everyone. Join hands and close your eyes."

The people on either side of me reached for my hands, and I panicked. I don't like to touch people. Sometimes, I see things. To be fair, it was usually innocuous things. But sometimes… Let's just say some people have darkness about them.

I don't like darkness. I guess most people don't.

Still, I wasn't exactly in a position to get up and leave, so, against my better judgment, I slipped both my hands in theirs.

Instantly, a barrage of images shot through my

mind. A kitchen table with a stack of chairs forming an impossible tower. A metal bedframe rattling violently, the finials spinning illogically. Dishes flying off the shelves. Doors banging open.

I gasped.

*Poltergeists?*

I snapped my head from side to side, looking at the people to my left and right. I couldn't tell whom the images came from. Both people were frowning at me, brows furrowed. I didn't want to cause a scene, but one of these people had experienced poltergeist activity, and that just wasn't normal.

Suddenly, I had a bad feeling about this.

"Gathered here tonight are friends and loved ones, mortals seeking the immortal, the faithful seeking that upon which we place our faith." Andromeda was speaking again, swaying to a tune only she could hear. "Tonight, we call out into the void to seek one Miss Caitlin Pratchett, beloved mother of…?"

Andromeda looked to the man in question, her eyebrow cocked. He nodded. "Chase Pratchett," he said.

"Beloved mother of Chase Pratchett. We come in perfect love and trust and open our hearts to you. Ms. Caitlin Pratchett, if you have a message for your son, please share it now. Begin by letting us know you hear and accept our invitation."

The room was deathly still as we collectively held our breath. I'd never been to a séance before, so I didn't know what to expect. Still, I expected *something*—a voice or a crack of lightning at least.

But nothing happened.

With my eyes closed, I could only gauge the others' reactions by listening to their breathing and the squeak of the chairs as they shifted in their seats. Someone let out the smallest of sighs. Was it disappointment? Or maybe fear?

"Caitlin Pratchett," Andromeda said, louder. "If there is such a being as Caitlin Pratchett, I bid you appear before us with an indication that you hear and accept our invitation!"

The woman at my right closed her hand more firmly in mine. The man to my left breathed in sharply through his nose.

Otherwise, the room was silent.

Too silent.

I chanced opening my eyes just a slit. Andromeda sat in the flickering darkness, eyes still closed, a perplexed frown on her face. "Perhaps you should try speaking, Chase." Andromeda said. "Is there a question you'd like to ask your mother?"

With a sharp inhale, Chase Pratchett spoke. "Mother, are you there? Sometimes I feel your presence. Are you watching over me? Are you watching over Rachel?" He stopped speaking abruptly, and I thought I heard his voice catch as emotion caught him off guard.

But Chase's plea was met only with an eerie silence.

"Everyone, please open your eyes. Perhaps we'll come back to you," Andromeda said softly. "Is there anyone else who wishes to speak with a loved one?"

"I know." At the other end of the table, Tamora leaned forward onto her elbows, placing her chin atop clasped hands. "Why don't we see if we can talk to Pride's family? I think everyone here would love to know what happened to Sam Lovelace's vanished commune."

———

I gazed at Andromeda, my heart in my throat. "I don't have any personal effects of theirs," I stammered. "I don't even know their names."

Andromeda leaned her head to the side and offered me a lopsided smile. "That's certainly a challenge. I prefer to address the dead by name, while in possession of a personal item. But in this case, we'll have to make an exception."

I didn't want to make an exception. I wanted to turn this séance around and go home, but then Andromeda's back stiffened, and her shoulders squared. "All right, everyone. Let's try again. Please close your eyes. Think about that lost commune, the poor souls who disappeared into thin air and were never seen again. Please hold in your mind the image of the sole survivor of that mysterious incident— Pride, discovered as a wee babe. Let us hold these thoughts in our minds as we try to access the dearly departed."

The man and woman at my sides squeezed my hands tighter, and I swallowed down my objections, an icy chill running down my spine. I didn't know what else to do, so I closed my eyes and let my chin drift to my chest. Andromeda's words filled my ears.

"Spirits of the great beyond, we call out with a most unusual request. We have no name and no personal effects. But as we sit with Pride today, we beseech the very people who brought this lovely person into the world. If you're there, please let us know."

Silence stretched for several agonizing moments. Then, just as I thought maybe I would be spared, a cold draft whistled through the room, fluttering through my hair. My skin pimpled over, and I opened my eyes, searching the room. The other guests' eyes were open, too, their bodies held taut, their faces frozen.

The candles on the table stuttered and then went out.

A collective gasp went around the room. No sooner had smoke begun to rise from the extinguished flames that the table started to shake. The temperature dropped, and the table jerked violently to the right, screeching loudly as it scraped across the floor and then lifted into the air.

I sat in stunned silence as the table levitated, climbing higher and higher before my eyes.

Throughout the library, something else was happening. Books tumbled from their shelves, spines cracking as they landed haphazardly on the hardwood floor. A sound like thunder cracked through the room as the darkness above our heads split open to reveal a pool of eerie blue light dotted with white. It shimmered and danced, undulating.

At the head of the table, a voice spoke into the darkness.

"Find some of all profits," the voice said.

I turned my head, blinking in surprise and—I admit it—absolute terror. Andromeda's head was tilted back, and her mouth hung open, her eyes rolled to the back of her head. Her cloud of pink hair floated from her shoulders, fanning around her like a cotton candy halo. The voice was coming from her body, but it wasn't her voice.

I couldn't place it. And yet, somewhere in the pit of my soul, I recognized it. It was as familiar to me as my own name, something I heard long, long ago, and it plucked my heart strings. Another chill ran down my spine.

"Find some of all profits on vinyl," the voice repeated. "Start there. That's where you began. Some of all profits on vinyl."

Then Andromeda's head snapped forward, and her eyes opened wide, her gaze trained on me. Whoever or whatever had taken over the medium's body was staring holes into my skull, and my skin crawled under the scrutiny. I'm garbage at reading people's faces, especially possessed people channeling spirits of the dead.

But I think the expression Andromeda's hijacked face wore was astonishment.

She lurched to her feet and grabbed me by the shoulders. Then, in a hushed voice, she said, "Sam warned us this might happen."

Then Andromeda's face fell slack, and she collapsed at my side.

The table crashed to the floor, knocking the candles on their sides. They rolled to the edge, spilling wax across the table's surface before clattering to our feet. The overhead pool of light vanished. The aftermath of the chaos was frightening in its stillness.

Finally, Tamora released the hands of the guests at

her sides. I snatched my own away as well, dropping them in my lap. Tamora stretched her fingers and adjusted the thin straps of her slip. "I think that's all for tonight," she said, her Cheshire Cat grin growing ever wider, her eyes never once leaving my face.

# four

. . .

"You set me up."

The four of us were alone in the library. Tamora had sent everyone else home and was now sitting at the table, smiling at me. Wrath and Andromeda were still seated as well, wearing twin looks of confusion. I was on my feet, trembling with fury, an accusing finger pointed in Tamora's face.

"You set me up," I repeated. "Did the network put you up to this?" I whirled on my heel to face Wrath. "Were you in on this?"

Scowling, Wrath held up his hands, palms out. "Man, I had nothing to do with this. From my perspective, this whole thing was a giant waste of time."

Andromeda sat silently at the head of the table. She'd woken up, but she looked drowsy, like she wasn't fully back in her body yet. "Please stop shouting," she said, her fingers pressed against her temples. "Could I please get some water?"

"Good luck with that," Wrath said. "I've been asking for water since we got here."

I studied Andromeda, my blood still boiling. She wore a grimace, eyes squeezed shut. She didn't *look* guilty, not like someone who had just exploited a stranger's past for her own amusement.

Though, to be fair, Tamora didn't look remorseful, either.

She looked delighted.

At least one of us was amused.

"I did set you up," Tamora said finally. "When Bailey said you were coming out to the house to investigate my—how did she put it? My catfishing case?—I knew I had to do something. I wasn't going to let you come into my house and try to make me look like a fool. Plus, how many opportunities does a person have to investigate one of the most famous disappearances of our time? When you look at it like that, it would be a sin *not* to set you up."

"It was cruel and unnecessary," I said. I was too amped up to sit down, so I paced around the room, stepping over candles and heaps of books. "You could have just *asked* me. You could have—"

"You would have said no, and anyway, that wasn't the point. You wanted to humiliate me. I wanted to humiliate you first."

"I *never* wanted to humiliate you!" I shouted. "I don't even know you! I just wanted to do the job I was hired to do. Your sister thinks you need to be protected from a charlatan after your fortune. But you know what? Now that I've met you, maybe it's the rest of *us* who need to be protected from *you!*"

"Oh, *do* keep shouting," she cooed, fluttering her lashes. "You're *very* pretty when you're angry."

If the cameras weren't filming, I think I might have slapped that smile right off her face. I'm not usually a violent person, but Tamora Preston was pushing all my buttons.

I turned to Andromeda. "I suppose you were in on it as well?"

The medium blinked, slowly coming out of her haze. She crossed her arms over her chest, her eyes cut into narrow slits. "I came out of retirement for this," she said. She shot a dark glance at Tamora as well. "Tamora told me you'd be here. And I admit, I wanted to see if I could channel your family. On my own, it would have been impossible, not to mention unethical. With you here, we at least had a chance. But I had no idea you didn't volunteer for this. I'm sorry about that."

"You have nothing to apologize for," Tamora said. She climbed to her feet and walked to the other end of the table. She slid into an empty seat next to Andromeda and placed her hand on top of the medium's. "Something happened here tonight. You channeled something. Some*one*. For decades, no one has made any progress toward finding that missing commune. Tonight, we received a clue. A precious clue!"

I stared at her. "What clue? What are you *talking* about? The table flew around, the books and candles fell to the ground, and the bloody ceiling turned into a lake of light but how is any of that a clue?"

"Are you dumb?" Tamora was looking at me as though she truly questioned my mental state. "Didn't you hear what Andromeda said when she was under?"

My jaw clenched. "Find some of all profits on vinyl? How is that a clue? It doesn't even make sense!"

"Not that," Tamora whined, growing impatient. "'Sam said this might happen.' She meant Sam Lovelace! It was his commune!"

Wrath looked just as confused as I felt. "How is that a clue? Sam said *what* might happen? Hang on, why are we even talking about this? We're supposed to be talking about *your* dead husband!"

"Please, everyone, stop." Andromeda shrank back into her chair, withdrawing her hand into her lap. "I don't know what happened here tonight," she said. "I didn't see it, and I won't understand it until I watch the footage." She jutted her chin in the cameraman's direction. "You'll turn over the footage to me before you edit or release any of it," she instructed. "I haven't signed any release form, and I'm not afraid to sue your network into the ground if any of this gets leaked. You understand?" She returned her attention to Tamora. "But you shouldn't have tried to channel a loved one without consent. Regardless of what may or may not have happened. That was wrong."

My anger was already fading—it was never an emotion I liked the cling to. But as my fury dwindled, something else began gnawing at me. "This doesn't make sense," I said. "Your sister said you've been talking to someone online who claims to be your dead husband trapped in another person's body. Right?"

Tamora stiffened, obviously taken aback by the change in subject. Good. Let her be uncomfortable. "That's right," she said.

"So if you have access to the world's greatest psychic medium," I gestured toward Andromeda, "why use her to play a trick on *me?* Why not take advantage of her talents to find out the truth? All you have to do is channel your husband's spirit. If he's not trapped in someone else's body, he should make an appearance, right?"

Tamora sat back in her chair, crossing her legs at the knee and shaking her head. "You don't understand," she said. "I don't need proof. I've been talking to this person online for six months. I know what I felt. I know what I experienced. I'm not talking to a fake. I'm talking to Jeff."

"How on earth can you possibly know that?" I exclaimed.

"He knows things only Jeff would know," she said, her voice suddenly breaking with emotion. "Moments we shared. Things I said to him. There's no way those things could be faked. It's Jeff. I know it is."

"He could have told *anyone* those things before he died," I said.

"He would never," she said. "Jeff was very private. Especially where I was concerned."

"Why not just test it?" Wrath was also on his feet now, pacing around the room like I was. "Have Andromeda channel him and see what happens. If he shows up, he's not stuck in anyone's body and you can get on with your life. If he doesn't show up…" He shrugged. "At least you'll have data. So why don't you do that? You have nothing to lose, right?"

"That's where you're wrong." Tamora wasn't looking at either Wrath or me. She was peering at Andromeda. "Let's say Andromeda successfully channeled Jeff. What if he gets stuck again? I can't very well marry Andromeda, can I?"

I stopped pacing, gaping at Tamora, incredulous. "What? He might get stuck *again?* Tamora, what if he never got stuck in the first place? Isn't it more likely your husband is on the other side, enjoying his afterlife, and whoever you've been talking to is just *lying to you?*"

"It's *not* more likely," Tamora insisted. "He's *trapped in someone else's body!* I've heard his voice. How do you explain that? It's Jeff's voice on the phone!"

"This is getting us nowhere," Wrath said. He jammed his knuckles into his eyes, rubbing them wearily. "Andromeda, maybe you can talk some sense into her."

"I've never heard of a spirit getting trapped in a medium's body," the psychic said slowly, "but that doesn't mean it can't happen. If I tried to channel a spirit residing in an earthly host, probably nothing would happen. But it's *possible* it could be disastrous, both for the spirit and the host. We just don't know. And frankly, I'm not interested in proving anything to anyone. I only work with people who want my help. Live and let live is what I say."

Tamora's black-painted lips broke into a smile, but there was no warmth in it. "You and my sister are the ones who need proof," she said to me. "I have something better than proof. I have faith." She placed the flat of her palm against her chest as she said this. "It doesn't matter what you think. It certainly doesn't matter what Bailey thinks. And although all of you would love to discredit me and my experience, I know what I have with Cecil is the real thing."

Wrath and I replied in unison. "*Cecil?*"

Tamora's grin widened. "Yes. That's his name. The host, I mean. Jeff is trapped in Cecil's body. And although on paper I'll be marrying Cecil, I'll really be marrying Jeff."

In the years I'd worked with the San Diego Police Department as a paranormal investigator, I'd come across many unhinged people. But I'd met nobody who believed their dead husband was hanging out in someone else's body and was willing to marry a stranger to reunite with their spouse.

I mean, you just can't make this stuff up. RealTV Productions was definitely getting their money's worth.

"So that's it then? You just don't want to know the truth." Wrath plopped down in a chair, slouching, legs spread wider than necessary. I think they call it manspreading. "Look, man, that's fine and everything. That's your right. But you know we're gonna look into this with or without you, right? This is our challenge, man. And you may not want our help, but *I* want to win. So for me, this isn't about you at all."

Tamora sniffed disdainfully. "Believe me, Wrath, I was never under the misconception that it was." She rose to her feet, making shooing motions with her hands.

"Do whatever you like," she said. "Reverse search Cecil's phone number. Message his friends on Facebook. I draw the line at trying to channel him, though. Do you understand? I *do not consent* to that. Am I clear?"

Given what she had just done to me, I thought it pretty rich that she was refusing consent, but I just shrugged. "Whatever."

"And do me one favor," she continued. "When your investigation leads you to the same conclusion that I've already reached? That Jeff and Cecil are one and the same? Have the backbone to come back here and tell me to my face. Admit you were wrong."

I almost laughed at that. I didn't get cast as Pride for nothing. Admitting I was wrong on national television? Fat chance of that.

But I didn't have to say anything because Wrath answered for both of us. "You got a deal," he said, rising to his feet. "I guess we might as well get out of here."

We were halfway to the door when I stopped and turned. "I have one question before we leave. Who were those people who sat next to me tonight?"

Tamora squinted, thinking. "The man was Balthazar Andros. The woman was Victoria Webster. Why?"

I hesitated. The ethics around psychic revelations aren't exactly clear-cut. "I saw something when I held their hands. I'm not sure who the visions came from, but I saw evidence of poltergeists. Stacked chairs, dishes flying around the kitchen." I shrugged. "Might have been nothing."

Slowly, Tamora walked to where I stood, her eyes locked on mine. "Who put you up to this?" she asked.

I blinked, confused. "Excuse me?"

"The poltergeists," she said. "You said you saw *poltergeists*. The chairs and the dishes. What else did you see?"

I floundered, racking my memory for the exact images that had come. "A brass bedframe rattling. Doors being thrown open, things like that." I narrowed my eyes at her. "Why?"

Tamora sucked in a long breath. "Those were Jeff's memories," she whispered. "He was tormented by poltergeists growing up. How did you know that? Nobody knew that. How could you have seen that?"

"Somebody knew it," I said. "Either Victoria or Balthazar. Maybe one of them is the one catfishing you."

"Or one of them is Cecil," Wrath suggested, "and Jeff really is trapped inside that body."

I shot Wrath a dubious look. "You don't really believe that."

Wrath snorted and thumbed his nose. "Man, I'll believe anything if it gets me the votes. Now come on. It's late, and I'm still thirsty. Let's get a good night's rest, and in the morning, we'll go hunt down a dead guy."

# five

. . .

The next day, I found Sloth in the living room, lying on the couch. She was dressed in an old, ratty bathrobe and a pair of slippers that had long since needed to be retired. Her hair was in a messy bun, and a laptop was propped on her stomach. When she saw me, she waved lazily and scrubbed her face with her free hand. "Hey, Pride."

"Hey, Sloth," I answered. "What're you up to?"

Sloth frowned and gestured at the computer. "Me? Nothing. I mean, I was doing something, but I'm not getting anywhere. I'm too stupid to do detective work."

"Most people are," I said. "What are you investigating?"

Sloth heaved a sigh and sat up, shifting the computer into her lap. "Remember I told Mrs. Romanowsky I would help her find that organization her son was working with?"

I nodded. "Yeah, sure. I remember." As part of the last challenge, I'd stumbled upon a dead body. The victim was a loner named Walt Romanowsky. He was involved with an enigmatic organization that appeared to hunt down supernatural creatures. His mother had asked Sloth to find out what she could about them. "I told you I would help."

"Well, I got Walt's laptop from Mrs. Romanowsky," she said, gesturing to the machine in her lap, "and I've been looking through these emails. But none of it sounds suspicious at all. I found his exchange with somebody at Chenoweth," she said. Chenoweth International was supposedly the name of the organization we were investigating. "But it's just dumb *guy* stuff."

"Dumb guy stuff? What do you mean?"

Sloth patted the cushion next to her, and I plopped down at her side. She handed me the computer. "Here. Look. This is what I found so far. Like I said, maybe I'm just too stupid to understand what I'm looking at. But none of this has anything to do with hunting bounties."

I clicked on Walt's inbox, and the first thing I noticed was that it was surprisingly empty. He had a few confirmation emails from local retailers, some general newsletter spam, and quotes on car insurance. (That lizard wanted to save him 15%.) But I didn't see a single inbound message from Chenoweth.

Walt kept a meticulous inbox. Good for him; bad for us.

"Did you look in the sent folder?" I asked.

Sloth nodded. "Yeah, that's where I found the dumb guy stuff. I mean I'm stupid, but I'm not *that* stupid."

"You're not any kind of stupid," I answered absently. I clicked open the sent folder and began browsing.

Unlike the inbox, which was squeaky clean, it looked like he'd never scrubbed his this one. Most of his outgoing messages were sent to Ghost@Chenoweth-ITL.com.

I clicked the most recent one.

It read:

"Hey Ghost,

Haven't heard back from you. I still have your SuperHawks. If you can't pick them up, I can bring them to you. Otherwise, I'll have to transfer them to another garage. You know how it is; gotta make space for new customizations. Get back to me,

-Walt"

I glanced at Sloth. "What's a SuperHawk?"

"According to the internet, it's a motorcycle," she said.

"Oh, so that's what you meant by dumb guy stuff."

She nodded. "Uh huh."

I opened the next email in the list, which chronologically was actually a previous email. It read:

"What's up, Ghost!

So, I've got your Honda SuperHawks ready. I gotta say, they look sweet! I gave them new wheels and repainted them, so they look brand new—you won't even recognize them. I've got them locked up in my garage, so everything is secure. When do you want to come pick them up?

-Walt"

I clicked through about half a dozen other messages. It was more of the same. The recipient of his emails changed—Ghost, Jackal, Wolverine, etc.—but the gist was always the same. Your bike is ready, please come get it.

"Did his mom or anyone say anything about him doing motorcycle customization?" I asked.

Sloth shook her head. "No. But then again, we didn't ask, did we?"

"I guess not," I agreed. "Well, you're not stupid. I don't know what to make of these emails either. Unless…"

I switched tabs and ran a Google search for Chenoweth International. Their website was the first search result, and I clicked it.

It was a website for motorcycle customization enthusiasts. The site was a mixture of upcoming shows and events, with articles about motorcycle repair, maintenance, and customization. Apparently, they held conferences and workshops all over the world. There was even a store section. I clicked **SHOP**, and a pop-up informed me the store was members only. I could either log in or request an account.

"Let's see if we can log in as Walt," I suggested. His email address was already populated on the login screen. I clicked "Reset password" and received a notification that someone would get back to me within 10 business days with a new password.

"It's not automated?" Sloth asked with a frown. "An actual *person* has to reset our password?"

"Looks like it," I said. "Well, I guess that's all we can do with this for now. Though it is *weird*."

"The password thing *is* weird," Sloth agreed.

"Not that. I was in Walt's bedroom. He had tons of paintings of animals but nothing about motorcycles."

"To be fair," Sloth said, "he's a grown man. What grown man puts up pictures of motorcycles in his bedroom?"

"The kind of grown man who lives at home with his mother?"

Sloth hrmmed, nodding. "Okay, fair point. Still, we don't know *anything* about him. Not really. Maybe his mom was wrong. Maybe there's nothing nefarious about Chenoweth after all."

"*Maaaybe*," I drawled. But even though I saw where Sloth was coming from, things weren't adding up in my mind. The cops found handcuffs on Walt's body. In addition, they'd found a cat carrier at the scene of his death which was presumed to belong to him. Of course, neither of these things meant he was a supernatural bounty hunter. But his mom claimed he was a member of a secret organization, and Walt's good friend Charmaine confirmed it, saying the organization hunted supernatural bounties.

These two women were the closest people to Walt in the world. Could they both be wrong?

Maybe, maybe not. Either way, I wouldn't know more until Walt's password on the Chenoweth website was reset.

I handed the laptop back to Sloth. "I wish I could be more help," I said. "but I need to get going. Wrath and I have an appointment. Will you be around later? Maybe we can grab a bite to eat."

"We'll see," Sloth said, returning to her previously prone position on the couch. I noticed her bathrobe had at least three new fresh stains. "I'm pretty tired."

"Suit yourself," I said. "I'll look for you when I'm back. If you look halfway presentable, I'll treat you to ice cream."

Sloth smiled sleepily. "Thanks, Pride. I can see what Lust sees in you. You treat everyone like they matter."

I paused, frowning. "Everyone does matter," I said.

Her smile faltered, and she looked away. "You're pretty much the only person I've ever met who really believes that."

———

"Is this the place?"

I checked the address on the building against the address pulled up on my phone and nodded. "Looks like it," I said. "Not exactly what I expected."

Our appointment today was with Balthazar Andros, the guy who'd been sitting next to me at Tamora's séance. He was apparently some kind of shamanic healer. He must be doing pretty well for himself. The office was in a posh, upscale building.

Wrath shook his head, killing the engine. "I expected something more, you know, down to earth? Homey? Isn't this guy supposed to be a New Age consultant or something?"

"Whatever that means," I agreed. "To be honest, I didn't read that much about him on his website."

Wrath and I got out of the car and headed towards the building looming before us. We checked the directory in the lobby, confirming our destination. I pointed to Balthazar's name. "Third floor."

Three floors up, we walked into Balthazar's office, and a chill ran down my spine. There was nothing wrong with the place, strictly speaking. A plump receptionist sat behind the desk where we signed in. The waiting area was mostly empty except for a few anxious-looking people thumbing through magazines, checking their phones, and perusing the various pamphlets available.

That's when I realized what was bothering me. Balthazar's office reminded me of Dr. Xena's office. My therapist. The therapist I hadn't seen in months. So that wasn't a chill running down my spine.

That was guilt.

I was too nervous to sit, but Wrath took a seat next to a middle-aged woman holding a pamphlet. The title was, "Losing Weight After Menopause: A Guide to Mid-Life Beauty." He gestured at her reading material and said, "You know, diet culture is a tool of the patriarchy."

The woman looked up and blinked. "Excuse me?"

"These people are only trying to make you think you have a problem so they can sell you a solution," he said. "Who made them an authority on what you should look like? Do you think it's just rotten luck that men supposedly get better looking as they age while women don't? That's nonsense, man! It's based on the idea that women have to be young to be valuable. It's breeder propaganda. You look great. Don't let anybody tell you different."

The woman blushed bright crimson and set the pamphlet aside. "Thanks, but I'm not trying to lose weight for my looks. I'm doing it for my health."

Wrath rolled his eyes and leaned forward, dangerously close to invading the poor woman's personal space. "Losing weight for your *health?* Do you know what a load of hogwash that is? Look, man. You can be totally healthy and fat. I'm not saying you're fat. I'm just saying."

I cleared my throat. "Wrath—"

"You gotta look at your *numbers,* man," he continued, ignoring me. "What does your cholesterol look like? What's your resting heart rate? How about your glucose? Those are the numbers to watch. Not the numbers on a scale. And don't get me started on BMI charts," he said, holding up his hand to stave off an objection that wasn't coming. The woman looked far too stunned to speak. "BMI charts were created by insurance companies, not health experts. BMI has nothing to do with your health! It's about maximizing profits."

"Wrath," I said, raising my voice a little. He was causing a scene, which was mortifying. "I don't know if now is the time for this."

But Wrath continued to ignore me. He was really on a roll. "Listen to me, man. If you want to lose weight because you have an idea in your head about what you want to look like – I guess that's fine. After all, if you told me you wanted to dye your hair pink or something,

I wouldn't try to talk you out of it, even though your natural hair looks great. Aesthetics are okay, man. It's cool to want to look a certain way. But *you* should decide what you look like! Come on, man. Doesn't this stuff tick you off?" He gestured to the now-abandoned pamphlet. "I know it ticks me off."

The woman looked at me, cheeks still flaming red. She gestured towards Wrath and adjusted in her seat. "Is he your friend?"

"Friend is maybe putting it too strongly," I said. "But he's with me."

Wrath sucked his teeth and rolled his eyes. "I'm not with anybody, man. I do my own thing. I'm just saying. If you're here to see that shamanic healer about losing weight? Rethink it is all I'm saying. Make up your own mind."

The woman hesitated a moment, fidgeting with her wedding band. Then, as though confirming something to herself, she gave a crisp nod, gathered up her things, and stood. "You know what? You're right. I'm not even sure I want to lose weight. It seems like such a hassle, but I thought…well, it doesn't matter what I thought. I guess I needed to hear that today."

Wrath jabbed a finger in the air. "Yeah, you did! Everybody needs to hear it sometimes. Truth to power, man. That's what I'm here for."

As the woman left, closing the door behind her, I slid into her spot, leaning in close to Wrath and lowering my voice. "Don't be too proud of yourself. I don't think you changed her mind. I think you freaked her out. Why do you do that? Why do you go on these crazy rants?"

"Somebody has to, man. I don't want to live in a society ruled by self-hatred and capitalism. Do you?"

I gestured around me. "Who is ruled by self-hatred and capitalism? We are literally sitting in a shaman's office. As things go, that seems pretty counterculture to me, don't you think?"

But Wrath folded his arms across his chest and leaned back, shaking his head in disgust. "A shamanic healer with weight loss pamphlets in his lobby, man. That dude needs to do some serious self-reflection."

I was about to open my mouth to suggest that maybe Wrath should take his own advice when the receptionist cleared her throat and waved us over. "Wrath? Pride? Balthazar will see you now."

I followed Wrath down the hall. At the end of the hall was a room cordoned off with a curtain. We pushed through it into a dimly lit space furnished with two low tables and a half dozen floor cushions. Balthazar sat on one of the two cushions flanking a small brazier. Flames licked the bottom of a stone bowl that rested on coals.

"Welcome in," he said. "Please, make yourselves comfortable."

Since there were no chairs, we were forced to choose floor cushions, and though we took our seats, I don't know that I'd go so far as to say I was comfortable. Here's why:

1.  I wasn't sure anyone should be lighting fires
    in an office building. That seemed like it
    would be against the lease, at least.

2. Balthazar looked so different than he had at Tamora's. Instead of a suit and tie, he wore a pair of sweatpants pushed up to his knees and his broad, deep brown chest glistened with sweat. His dreadlocks were pulled into a neat ponytail, and he wore a purple paisley bandanna on his head.

3. Sitting on the floor just isn't what it's cracked up to be.

I felt like I was at some kind of culturally appropriated sweat lodge, and I was way, way outside my comfort zone.

Balthazar hunched over the brazier, reaching into the flame and coaxing it with a pair of iron tongs. As he did, the coals shifted, and a strange odor filled the room.

"Please, not more incense," Wrath complained. He turned to me. "What is it with this town and incense?"

Balthazar grinned and put the tongs aside. "It's not incense, strictly speaking," he said. "This is chamomile, St. John's Wort, and Holy Basil. These are herbs I use for their ability to uplift the spirit. It has a balancing effect on the mental body. I'll be using this cleansing rite to purify the pathways of your being so I can better understand the nature of your concerns."

"The pathways of our being are already pure, thanks," Wrath said, inching away from the coals. "Can you put that out? Seriously, we just want to talk. We've had enough voodoo for a lifetime."

Balthazar chuckled, his grin widening. "This isn't voodoo, but sure, I understand. My patients usually appreciate the more spiritual approach." He put a lid on the bowl.

"Well, we're not patients," Wrath said. "We want to talk to you about poltergeists."

Balthazar leaned back on his wrists and studied us, his smile faltering. "Poltergeists," he repeated. When neither of us said anything, he sighed, the smile slipping away completely. "You're gonna need to explain that."

I told Balthazar everything I knew, which wasn't much. I explained Bailey's suspicions, Tamora's attitude, and the experience I had when I touched him and Victoria at the séance. When I finished, the shaman rubbed his hands together, eyes narrowed in thought.

"Wow, that's a lot. Can I ask you something stupid?" he asked.

"You seem capable," I said.

The slightest smile cracked over Balthazar's face. "I've been practicing the metaphysical arts for a long time. I've helped people overcome addictions and heal childhood scars. I've mended broken people and helped them tackle new life adventures. But in all my time, I've never seen any proof of life after death. I think that's why I help people achieve their potential here and now. We're not promised tomorrow."

He stopped talking long enough for me to think he was done, but he hadn't actually asked a question. I kept waiting, but he kept on not saying anything. Finally, I said, "Is there a question in here somewhere?"

Balthazar laughed, a full sound that rumbled in my belly. "Sorry, yeah. I guess I just want to know what you know. What happens after we die?"

"I have no idea," I said simply.

The shaman blinked. "Really? But you said you were a ghost whisperer."

"I am," I agreed. "I see ghosts. That doesn't mean I have the answers to life, the universe, and everything. I mean, what about you? You were at the séance. If you don't believe in life after death, what were you doing there?"

Balthazar hrmmed and placed his hands lightly on his knees. He straightened his back, tipping his chin up to the ceiling. "You want to know the truth? I'm not sure. I told myself it was research. But that's only half the truth. I was also curious about Andromeda Clark. I wanted to see her do her thing in person."

"And what did you think?" Wrath asked.

"I don't know," the shaman admitted. "It didn't go the way I expected."

"That makes two of us," I growled under my breath.

"It was scary," Balthazar continued. "The way the table levitated and the books fell and everything. It makes me wonder, though. Why would that happen? Why would a spirit's appearance cause such a disruption? It never happened that way on Andromeda's show," he pointed out. "In fact, she never used rituals. She just invited a spirit into her body, and it showed up. So why the theatrics? Why a séance at all?"

These were valid questions. But like everything else Balthazar had asked today, I had no answers.

Balthazar breathed in sharply and shook himself as though casting the memory aside. "Anyway, you didn't come here to hash all that out. Back to the matter at hand, then. Can you tell me more about poltergeists in general? Are they evil ghosts? Angry beings in life that became angry beings in death?"

"Well, no. Poltergeists aren't ghosts," I explained. "Ghosts are spirits of dead people. Poltergeists are something else. There's an entire world beyond what you or I can see or experience. It's out there. I didn't even know wights existed until I moved to Odyssey and encountered them at Wights and Wongs. But sure, poltergeists exist. Whether they're angry, I don't know. They throw things. They make a lot of noise. They scare the bejesus out of people who live with them, but they're not ghosts. They're their own thing."

"I see. Is there a reason a person would attract a poltergeist? I'm sorry I have so many questions. But you don't run into this every day."

"That's true," I agreed, "but to be honest, I don't know. I'm not an expert in paranormal activity. Just ghosts."

The shaman looked disappointed, but he was good-natured about it, shrugging and smiling. "Ah. Well, sorry, then. I just thought I'd ask. So, tell me. What does any of this have to do with Jeff?" Balthazar asked.

"I was hoping you could tell me," I said. "Tamora said those were his memories. I don't know what to make of that. Usually, when I touch people, I see their most emotional moments. The death of a pet, getting their first big job, a wedding, things like that. But I've never touched a person and seen someone else's memories."

The shaman was quiet for a while, staring down at

the burning embers. He lifted the lid from the bowl, and a thick pillar of smoke billowed out. Wrath coughed loudly, burying his nose in the crook of his arm. But Balthazar leaned forward and breathed the smoke in deeply. I bet his lungs were just garbage by now.

"I started working with Jeff about 18 months before the climb," he said finally, replacing the lid. "I was quite surprised when he came to me for help. I knew about him, of course. Big-time philanthropist, often in the news, you know. Plus, when he moved down here, the city council made a big deal about it. They used his name in their advertising for the various real estate properties for sale. So when he came to my office, it caught me off guard. I didn't figure him for the spiritual sort."

I quirked an eyebrow at that. "Any reason?"

Balthazar waved a hand, dismissing my question. "Oh, you know how it is. People with money often come off as soulless, you know?"

"They come off that way because they *are* that way," Wrath interjected. "Money makes people into monsters. Life becomes all about winning, and the winner is the one with the biggest cash pile. It's the worst blight we suffer from as humans. Left unchecked, capitalism will destroy—"

"Maybe we can talk about this later," I interrupted, throwing Wrath a remonstrative look. He scowled but clamped his mouth shut, looking away.

I returned my attention to Balthazar. "You were saying?"

"Jeff's reasons for coming to me were twofold. The

first part was physical training. He wanted to learn how to breathe properly to maximize his oxygen efficiency. There's a spot up there called the death zone where people really suffer physically. Their brains and lungs are starved for oxygen, and the body begins to die. The mind plays tricks, and they become psychotic. They hallucinate people who aren't there. Things like that. Jeff wanted to be prepared. His physical training included the basics like calisthenics, but it also included body and mind purification. I taught him how to breathe and what to eat for optimum performance. We based his regimen around his astrological sign and blood type."

Wrath and I exchanged looks. Look, just because someone has money doesn't mean they can't buy into bunk science, okay? Money makes you rich. It doesn't make you a genius.

"But aside from the physical, there was a spiritual aspect to his visits, too. I don't really know how to explain it, and if I'm honest, part of me feels like discussing this with you might be an ethical breach. Doctor-patient confidentiality and all," he said with a weary smile.

I stared at the shaman through the smoke. "Good thing you're not a doctor," I said.

Balthazar stiffened. "I have a Ph.D. in holistic healing."

"My baby cousin has a driver's license from a Cracker Jack box, too, man, but it wouldn't hold up in court," Wrath interjected sharply.

I turned to Wrath and pressed a finger to my lips,

giving him the best *Can you please shut up and let the guy talk?* look I could muster. Again, Wrath turned away in a huff.

Balthazar was silent for a long stretch, and I worried Wrath had cost us the rest of the interview. But finally, he took a deep breath and let it out in a loud exhale. "Jeff had his fair share of demons. I guess we all do. He spoke little of his childhood. He was very private that way. But he credits his parents with instilling philanthropic ideals in him from a young age. He had several foster siblings over the years. Still, his life was missing something. That's why he climbed Mount Everest. He needed to push his limits and see what it did for his soul. He came to me to learn what was possible up there."

"Possible in what way?"

The shaman groped for the right words, searching for a way to explain. "It's kind of like when you go to the symphony," he said finally. "Beautiful music is beautiful music, and you don't need to know a thing to appreciate the notes. But when you understand more—world events that inspired the music, the composer's love life or living situation, things like that—it adds another dimension to your appreciation. For instance, knowing Beethoven was deaf makes the marvel of his music even more profound. That's what Jeff wanted from me. Context. He wanted to understand the spirit better, so he'd know what to look for when he reached the top of that mountain."

"Which he never reached," I said.

Balthazar nodded, the corners of his mouth falling

into a frown. "Which he never reached," he agreed. "It was a blow to the community, losing Jeff. He was such a wonderful man. Admittedly, we were all baffled by his relationship with Tamora. They were very different, those two. But the more distance I get from his death, the more I believe he wanted to save her."

Now, I cocked my head to the side, blinking in the dim light. My eyes still burned from the smoke. "Save Tamora? How? From what?"

Balthazar sucked his teeth. "You've been to her house," he said. "She has an unhealthy relationship with darkness and death. An unhealthy relationship with the metaphysical—and that's coming from me. What kind of woman relies on séances and mediums to make even the most basic decisions in life? She's broken. I don't know why or how—that's between her and her maker. But I think Jeff saw that and wanted to fix her, so he had to fix himself first."

This was a lot of information, but I wasn't sure any of it was getting us closer to the answers we sought. "Okay. Well, back to the poltergeists," I said. "Did he ever talk to you about them? Do you know anything you can tell me?"

Balthazar just shook his head, his shoulders falling low. "I would tell you if I knew something," he said. "But Jeff never mentioned any poltergeists. If it happened when he was a kid, I'm not surprised he said nothing. Like I mentioned, he kept mum about growing up. Childhood and family were something he didn't like to discuss. I wish I could be more helpful. I really do. But that's all I know."

With some discomfort, Wrath and I climbed to our feet. My legs were tingling from sitting cross-legged for so long. I really needed to start doing yoga or something. "Thanks for your time," I said. "Maybe we'll see you around."

Balthazar led us out of the curtained area and back into the hallway, where we welcomed the smoke-free blaze of the fluorescent lighting. As we were leaving, the shaman placed a hand on Wrath's shoulder, stopping him. "You seem like someone who could benefit from spiritual advisement," he said. "I can help you release that anger. Teach you calming exercises. Think about it. The first session's on me if you'd like to come in."

Wrath offered a tight smile and thrust his hands into his pockets. "My anger keeps me alive," he said.

When we were outside and loaded into the car, I turned to Wrath. "Do you think you'll take Balthazar up on his offer?" I asked. "Maybe you can do a shamanic journey or something."

My housemate laughed, maybe the first real laugh I'd ever heard him utter. "Seriously, I think I'd rather set myself on fire, man."

I couldn't help but smile. Finally, something Wrath and I agreed on.

# six

. . .

"So, what should we do first?"

We were in Wrath's room back at the house, surrounded by his electronics. The cameraman was having trouble settling in and getting a good shot because of all Wrath's equipment. But every time the guy tried to arrange Wrath's things, Wrath slapped his hand and shouted at him in a language I didn't speak.

"By the way," I said as Wrath muttered something I didn't understand under his breath. "What language is that? Am I allowed to ask, or is that racist?"

"Vietnamese," he said. "Why would that be racist?"

"I don't know," I admitted, "but lots of things I don't recognize as racist actually are, and I don't want to be offensive."

"First of all, ignorance doesn't offend me, so don't worry about it. Ask me whatever, man. But secondly, you worry too much. It would be racist if you assumed I was speaking Chinese or if you asked me if I'm good at math. But it's not racist to be curious. You know what really ticks me off?"

"Everything," I answered earnestly.

"Well, right. But no. It ticks me off when people think ignoring differences is somehow progressive. It's nonsense, man. We're different. People, I mean, not you and me. Although you and me are pretty different. Where did you grow up, anyway?"

"Around here," I said. "San Diego."

"That's what I thought," Wrath muttered. "You seem comfortable here with these rich people and idiot charlatans like that shaman. You can't help how you grew up, man, so don't get defensive. But I grew up outside Salt Lake City. You know? Where the Mormons are."

I had no idea where he was going with any of this. "Are you Mormon?"

Wrath's eyes grew wide. "Do I look Mormon?"

I had no idea what Mormons were supposed to look like, but I wasn't so dense I didn't recognize his incredulity. "I guess not?"

"Of course not. Look, man, the point is, we're all different. We should celebrate those differences and learn from them. But anyway, I'm comfortable with charlatans, too. I grew up with them. Mine are just different from yours."

That seemed like an avenue of conversation rife with blind alleys I didn't want to turn down, so I changed the subject. "So, what should we do first?" I repeated.

"I guess we need to learn what we can about the guy pretending to be Jeff," Wrath said. "Here's all the info we have from Bailey Preston." He pointed to the computer screen, and an email from Bailey popped up listing everything she knew about the person Tamora was dating.

"He claims his name is Cecil Bradshaw from San Francisco. Let's look up his social media profiles."

Without anyone touching the keyboard, several new windows popped up in the browser. The first took us to a Facebook profile for Cecil Bradshaw in San Francisco. I pointed at it. "Is that him?"

"Looks like it," Wrath confirmed. "See, he's friends with Tamora Preston. Ok, this is a red flag."

I squinted at the profile, trying to see what Wrath had noticed, but everything looked normal to me. Not that I was an expert. I didn't have a Facebook page. It was too mortifying to post daily updates about banal minutiae, and I was absolutely not posting pictures of my meals, no matter how photogenic. "What is?"

Wrath gestured at the screen. "He's only got, like, 45 friends. A real profile would have in the hundreds."

I nodded like this made sense, but really, I was surprised. I didn't know forty-five people I cared enough about to follow on Facebook, so maybe Cecil didn't, either. But then I remembered I was the socially awkward weirdo on this cockamamie TV show, so maybe I wasn't the best judge of things like that. "So you think this profile is fake?"

Instead of answering, Wrath navigated away from the page, and a new browser window popped up. "Search the internet for photos of Cecil found on his Facebook page," he told the computer. "Show me anything that matches." He folded his arms across his chest. "If he took his profile photos from another website, we'll find them."

A moment later, a new window opened, and Wrath snapped his fingers in victory. "Man, that was too easy. Look at this, Pride." He clicked the first search result, and an image gallery popped up. "This guy didn't even *try*. This is an Instagram profile for—get this—a model from Israel named Amit Nagad." He tapped the screen to emphasize his point. As he scrolled down, my jaw dropped. Every picture he'd sent Tamora and every photo from his Facebook page were stolen from this Israeli model's page.

"But Amit Nagad has, like, *millions* of followers," I said, bewildered. "Who would be so stupid to steal photos from a popular profile like this?"

"Liars and charlatans are liars and charlatans," Wrath grumbled. "No one said they were mental prodigies."

"Okay, so it's obvious the person Tamora has been talking to isn't the person in the photos," I said, musing aloud. "So, what should we do next?"

Wrath scratched his head, thinking. "Well, I guess we have a couple options. Let's message some of his female Facebook friends and see if he's having a romantic relationship with any of them. If he's pulling a scam on Tamora, he may be pulling a scam on other people, too."

"That's a great idea," I said, rubbing my palms in excitement. "And if it turns out he's scamming other people, that should be enough to convince Tamora that he's a liar, right?"

Wrath scrubbed his face with his fingers and then swiveled in his chair to face me. "That's something I've been thinking about," he said. "You know, we actually have two different objectives. Bailey and the network want us to find out who's behind the profile. That's our challenge. But it's only half the battle. We still have another obligation, at least from my point of view."

I cocked an eyebrow. "What do you mean obligation?"

"I'm talking about justice, man. Doing the right thing. Tamora says she doesn't care who Cecil is, but if we can prove he's lying about having her husband's spirit stuck inside him, she'll cut him loose. Right? And I know that's not our challenge," he conceded, "but I couldn't live with myself if I let her continue a relation-ship with a charlatan. Even though she's a capitalist princess and I hate everything she stands for, I don't want anyone to take advantage of her, either. So, our challenge is to find out who Cecil is, but we *also* have to rescue Tamora."

As much as I hated to admit it, Wrath was right. "Okay, I see your point. But how do you propose we prove that this Cecil person is lying? I mean, not just about his profile picture and stuff. But about the things Tamora actually cares about."

"The only thing I can think of," Wrath said slowly, "is we have to get information out of him that only Jeff would know."

"And how are we supposed to find out something only Jeff would know?"

Wrath pointed a finger at me. "Exactamundo, man," he said. "I have no idea."

Wrath swiveled around again to face his computer. He folded his arms across his chest and leaned his head back. "Computer, I want to compose a message. Find all of Cecil Bradshaw's female friends and send them this note."

Wrath leaned forward and placed his fingers on the keys. "Easier if I just type this out myself," he said. "I feel like a jerk dictating an email message aloud."

The email message Wrath composed went like this:

"Hi there, <insert name here>,

I'm from a reality TV show called *Sinful House*. We investigate minor crimes for the locals in Odyssey, California, and solve mysteries the police are too busy to help with. Right now, I'm looking into this Cecil Bradshaw person—it looks like you're friends with him on Facebook. What can you tell me about him? Have you ever met him? Have you ever talked to him? And most importantly—are you in a romantic relationship with him? We think someone on our case might be getting catfished. I appreciate any help you can offer."

I read the email a couple times before nodding my approval. "I think that works," I said. "I can't believe we're actually doing this. This feels so... I don't know. Like high school? Like when someone would slip an anonymous note in your locker confessing their love and you had to figure out who it was."

Wrath shot me a sideways glance. "I definitely have no idea what you're talking about," he said.

I felt a flush creep up my neck. To be honest, I had no idea what I was talking about, either. Nothing like that had ever happened to me. But I'd seen it on television, so it must have happened to someone somewhere, right?

Don't answer that.

"Okay, let's move on. Bailey gave us all of Cecil's contact information, right? Should we look up his phone number?" I asked.

Wrath grunted. "Yeah, good idea."

A few moments later, Wrath pulled up the relevant information on the computer. According to the Internet, the phone number Cecil Bradshaw was using to talk to Tamora was registered to Cecil Bradshaw in San Francisco, California.

"Bollocks," Wrath swore. "It's his own phone number."

I picked up my phone. "Should we call him?"

Wrath grabbed my phone and laid it face down on the desk. "Not yet. We'll only get one chance to call him —then he'll be onto us. We should wait until we have more information."

"Okay…? What kind of information?"

Wrath ran his hands through his hair, mussing it from the roots. "Like where he really lives, if he's catfishing other girls, stuff like that. Cecil says he lives in San Francisco, which is where this phone is registered.

So that's a match. We need to find info that *doesn't* add up."

"True," I agreed, "but a phone number's not hard to fake. You could use one of those internet phone numbers."

"I guess. But right now, we have no reason to doubt this person lives in San Francisco, do we?"

"No," I drawled, "it's just that… Have you ever seen the movie *Silence of the Lambs?*"

Wrath made bug eyes at me and held out his hands. "Yes? Hasn't everybody seen that movie?"

"Right. Well, in it, Hannibal Lecter says something that stuck with me my whole life. He says something like, *We covet what we see every day.* I mean, let's say you're a conman looking to marry rich. You could catfish any number of women. If it were me, I'd target women with self-esteem issues. You know, someone desperate to be loved. Why go after someone like Tamora—who, let's face it, doesn't suffer self-esteem issues. And the even bigger question is—why pretend to be someone's deceased spouse? Doesn't that feel intensely personal? Like, really targeted?"

Wrath tipped his head back, nodding in thought. "Yeah. Yeah, maybe you're right. So you think this is someone she knows."

"Not necessarily," I said. "But someone who knows *her.*"

Wrath paused. "You think it's someone in Odyssey?"

I shrugged. "I don't know. Her dad was a big-time producer. Her husband was a famous philanthropist.

People all over know who she is. But still…this feels personal. I can't shake it."

"Well, trust your gut, I always say," Wrath said. He glanced down at his watch. "Hey, man, I gotta take a break. I'm starving."

"Sure. I've got some stuff I need to do, anyway."

Wrath wriggled his eyebrows and gave me a lascivious look. "Stuff? Or Lust?"

I snatched up my phone and kicked his chair before leaving his room.

Then I went to go look for Lust.

What can I say? I'm only human.

———

I searched the house for Lust, but she wasn't anywhere to be found. I didn't have anything I wanted to talk to her about or anything. I just missed her company.

Since I had some free time on my hands, I went down to the beach to soak up some sun and dip my feet in the water. In all the time I'd been at Sinful House, my trips to the beach had been few. First of all, the stupid cameraman followed me everywhere I went, and it's absolutely mortifying to be out in public with a camera following you around. I felt like a self-involved schmuck, and people stared at me. I don't know how vloggers do it. I really don't.

But aside from all that cameraman business, I grew up in San Diego. The beach wasn't exactly a novelty to me. It was, however, a place I liked to go to think. And right now, I had some thinking to do.

Initially, I'd agreed to come on the show because I didn't have much choice. I'd lost my job and my girlfriend and had nowhere to stay and no money. I let myself get invested in the show because whoever won America's Favorite Sin would win their heart's true desire. And so, for weeks, I grinned like a horse's ass for the cameras because I wanted my girlfriend back.

I wasn't so sure I wanted that anymore.

Don't get me wrong. It wasn't that I didn't love Shayda anymore. I did. I do. I'll probably feel that way about her forever. But I was beginning to think there was more to life than the love of one person. I hated to admit that something as corny as a *Sinful House* assignment got me thinking about it, but working on Tamora's case really did a number on me. Here was a woman who was obviously being swindled, and she couldn't even see it because she was so blinded by love for one person.

Look, I don't know much about anything. But even I know that's no way to go through life.

When I reached the shore, I rolled up the bottom of my pants and waded into the water, letting the sand squish through my toes. The water was cold and felt good on my hot skin. Overhead, seagulls circled, looking for fish. The beach was sparsely populated today, which made it easier to pick out the ghosts. There were only a handful out today, but still more than I expected. None of them were looking at me. They were lying in the sand, fully dressed in the clothes they'd died in, sunbathing.

I don't know if there's a ghost-specific term for lying

in the sun. Sunbathing doesn't sound right, but I don't know how else to describe it.

I was contemplating why ghosts would come to the beach at all when my phone rang.

"Hello?"

"Is this Sid Sheridan?"

I rubbed the back of my neck and looked around. I wasn't supposed to use my real name on the show, but then again, I guess the camera wasn't picking up the voice on the other end. "Yeah. Who's this?"

"Hello, Sid. This is Andromeda Clark."

I was so surprised, I just stood there like an idiot, mouth agape, saying nothing. After a moment, the voice on the other end said, "Hello? Are you still there?"

"I'm here," I said. "I'm just surprised, that's all."

"I guess that means you aren't the kind of psychic that sees the future."

"I'm definitely not," I admitted.

"So much the better, I say. Every movie would be ruined for you. And what would be the point of getting into a relationship? You'd already know how it was going to end. And the anticipation is the *entire* point!"

I hesitated. "The anticipation of a relationship ending is the point?"

"Well yes, depending on your point of view. Will it end after only seven weeks because you found out you can't stand the way he slurps his soup, or will he die at your side eighty years into the future? If you already know ahead of time which scenario you're walking into, it rather defeats the point of entering in at all, don't you think?'

I wasn't sure I agreed with any of that, but it was something to think about. Just not now. "Did you want something?"

"Of course. I didn't call you for my health. I wondered if you could make some time to speak with me."

I hesitated. "I am speaking with you now," I said matter-of-factly.

Andromeda laughed. "Yes. That's not what I meant. It's hard for me to hear you over the sound of the waves in the background. I hoped we might meet somewhere more intimate. Quieter. Would you be able to come to my hotel room? Sooner would be better than later," she amended.

I kicked at the sand and scratched my jaw. "Sure, I guess. I don't have any plans right now. Is now a good time?"

"Right now would be wonderful. I'm texting you my address. And please," Andromeda said. "I would appreciate it if you came alone. That means no cameramen and no sidekick. Understand?"

I glanced at the cameraman who was circling around me, no doubt trying to get the perfect shot of me against the sunlit ocean, wind in my hair, a slight burn on my nose. I did my best to keep my back to him. "I don't know if I can promise no cameras," I said. "But I'll do my best."

I didn't wait for a response before I disconnected.

# seven

. . .

Andromeda Clark's hotel room looked like a unicorn vomited all over it.

Not that it wasn't extremely classy. It was. It was just that it was absolutely overflowing with pink femininity. Dozens of bouquets of pink roses and peonies were scattered throughout the suite. The couches were stuffed with pink satin pillows, and pink candles covered nearly every flat surface. Pink throws and area rugs were layered over top of the hotel's banal décor.

Andromeda was wearing a fluffy pink bathrobe, her pink hair pulled away from her face in a high, messy bun. She was ensconced in the corner of one of her couches, her feet tucked into the crevices between the cushions. She was holding a champagne flute filled with pink champagne.

Like I said. Unicorn vomit. Everywhere.

"Do you drink champagne?"

I laid a hand on my chest and looked around. "Me?"

Andromeda giggled, her head cocked to one side. "I

wasn't speaking to the shadows. Why are you so jittery? Pour yourself a glass of bubbly and sit down with me."

I poured myself a glass of the pink champagne, and Andromeda scooted over, making room for me on the couch. I sat on the other end of the sofa, keeping a cushion's distance between us. I didn't want to invite too much intimacy. I couldn't imagine what might happen if I touched her skin. I might see anything.

And after what had happened the last time I met with her, I wasn't taking any chances.

"So," she said, smiling around the rim of her champagne glass. "We finally meet in private. The famous Sid Sheridan."

I felt my cheeks grow warm, and I took a sip of the champagne to hide my discomfort. "I wouldn't go so far as to call myself famous," I said. "I'm not exactly a household name."

"Well, but that's not true, is it? At least, you are very well known among people who study the occult and the metaphysical. People like myself. And people like Tamora."

I shifted uncomfortably, taking another sip from my glass. "Is that what you want to talk about? The commune? Because I have to tell you, I don't have much to say about that."

Andromeda peered at me, her lips pressed together as she considered my response. "We'll get to that. First, I want to talk about the séance. I watched the footage, you know. Helluva thing that happened."

I snorted. "You can say that again," I said. I looked up sharply, grinding my back molars. I hoped she wouldn't say it again. I really hated when people did that. It wasn't nearly as funny as they thought.

But Andromeda didn't say it again. Instead, she clucked her tongue against the roof of her mouth. "I've been doing this work for a long time," she said. "Are you familiar with my work? Did you ever watch the show?"

I nodded. "I've seen a few episodes." I don't know why I lied. I'd seen every episode at least once.

Andromeda hrmmed. "Then you know that isn't how I usually conduct business. I usually like to meet with people one on one and channel their loved ones into my body. No pomp, no circumstance."

"So why were things different at Tamora's? Why the séance?"

"That was for you," she said. "Well, not *for* you. It was *because* of you. Tamora told me you were coming, and she said you wanted to contact your family. I know she lied about that," Andromeda said, interrupting my prepared objection. "But I didn't know it at the time. Anyway, I knew my traditional methods wouldn't work under those circumstances. No one knows who your parents are, including you. And I knew you didn't have any of their personal effects. Lacking those very critical pieces of information, I thought it would be best to hold the séance. It creates more energy, helping the universe home in on our request. So that's why the séance. But even so."

She scooted towards me, so close I could smell her perfume. It was something fruity and overly feminine, like an upscale version of something you might find at Victoria's Secret. "All the theatrics with the books and the table? All of that is par for the course with any séance. So you have to look past all that. What struck me was that it *worked*."

My brow creased in confusion. "What do you mean, it worked? All I heard was nonsense."

Andromeda smiled, a soft stretch of her lips. "Nonsense words? Is that what you heard? Because I agree with Tamora about one thing: you got a clue to your past, Sid. 'Find some of all profits on vinyl'?" Unexpectedly, she took my free hand in both of hers, squeezing her fingertips against my knuckles. A thousand faces flashed before my eyes, each of them wanting something. Even the sight of it was exhausting.

"*On vinyl*, Sid. I think that means we're looking for a *record album*. A record album titled, *Some of All Profits.*"

I blinked. "That's plausible," I admitted. "Thanks for the tip."

Andromeda sat quietly for a moment. Then she said, "You don't seem…enthusiastic."

I hesitated, not wanting to hurt her feelings. She was obviously feeling chuffed that she'd figured this out on her own. But I wasn't nearly as excited as she was. "I am," I lied.

Andromeda pursed her lips and leaned in closer to me. "Sid, sweetheart, is this something you want to pursue?" she asked.

I shook my head, exhaling heavily. "No. It really isn't. I know everyone is cuckoo for Cocoa Puffs over the missing commune, but it doesn't interest me. Not in a personal way, anyway. My parents are dead. I'm on my own in this world. That's the only thing that matters."

Andromeda nodded, her expression growing soft and serious. "You're not really alone in the world, though, Sid. You have a tremendous light inside you. Others are drawn to it, and they'll accompany you on your journey if only you'll let them. Like the ghosts."

I stared at her. "The ghosts are drawn to me because I have a tremendous light inside me?"

Now, the psychic smiled, laughing. "Yes! Didn't you know that?"

"I didn't," I confessed.

"I see. I suppose there are a great many things you don't know. Not you in particular. But most of us are blind to our positive traits. Well, if you change your mind about pursuing your past, or if you need anything—"

"I do need something," I interrupted. I stood up to retrieve the champagne bottle and refreshed both glasses. "Did you know Jeff Bishop?"

Andromeda reached her hands into her hair and unwound her bun, letting her hair fall in billowing pink clouds around her shoulders. She massaged her scalp with her fingertips, eyes closed. "I've known the Prestons for decades," Andromeda began. "I met Adam Preston when I was just a young woman, new to the Hollywood scene. I'd just started gaining some notoriety, and Adam offered to help with my career. Not that I was a singer," she added with a laugh. "But powerful, famous people know other powerful, famous people, and he wanted to open doors for me. So I let him."

Andromeda reached for her champagne glass and took a deep sip. "I'm a few years older than Tamora, and in some ways, she treated me like an older sister. I wasn't as close with Bailey. See, Tamora has always been keen on the metaphysical, and I, obviously, have some insight in that arena. She relied on me for spiritual and psychic advice about everything—where to go to college, who to date, where to purchase a home. When Jeff proposed, she asked me if she should marry him. But I told her I didn't know."

The psychic sighed and set her glass on the table. "Jeff was a nice enough guy, don't get me wrong. But there was something about him I never could unlock. If I say he was secretive, it gives you the wrong idea. I don't think he was hiding things. It's just that he kept everything very close to his chest. He never talked much about himself. He never volunteered his thoughts and opinions. For a philanthropist, he didn't have many friends. Some people called him eccentric. I don't think that's accurate. It was more like Jeff was an anthropologist objectively observing the rest of the world without participating in it. Does that make sense?"

"I'm getting the picture," I drawled. "So you told Tamora you weren't sure about the marriage because you couldn't get a bead on him?"

Andromeda nodded. "Yes. That's exactly it. Of course, she married him anyway, and he made her very happy. Maybe he opened up to her over time. I don't know. But he certainly never opened up to me. I wish I could tell you who to talk to. Who might know him better. But I'm not sure anyone knew Jeff Bishop. Not really."

I cleared my throat and popped my knuckles. "Andromeda, do you know anything about poltergeists?"

Andromeda blinked. "Poltergeists?"

"Yes. Did Jeff ever mention them to you?"

The psychic sighed, shaking her head. "I don't know anything about that," she said.

I couldn't think of anything else to ask, so I finished the last of my champagne and got to my feet. "Thanks for all your help," I said. "I really appreciate it. And if I need anything else, I'll be in touch," I added.

"You do that," the psychic said, only a bare hint of a smile playing on her lips. "You do that."

———

Later that night, I was in bed reading a sci-fi novel when the temperature dropped, and a familiar sensation riffled over my skin. A small ghost climbed into bed with me, waving a hand in front of my face. I knew this ghost. I'd been seeing her ever since I was young. I grew up, but she never did. And she had a habit of showing up when I was least in the mood to deal with her.

I set the novel down with a sigh. "Can I help you with something?" I asked.

"Did you know cows sleep standing up?" she said.

I nodded. "Everybody knows that."

"Oh. Well, did you know some people are too stupid for their own good?"

I leaned my head back, tilting my face toward the ceiling. "If you have something to say, just say it."

"Andromeda wants to help you find your family."

The ghost said tersely. "You should let her."

"You know what's funny about you?" I asked. "You think you know things, but you actually don't know anything at all."

The ghost looked at me with wide eyes, her mouth falling open in disbelief. "Why would you say that? What are you talking about?"

I tucked my hands into my armpits and gave the ghost a stern look. "You don't know anything about how the world works. No, don't look at me like that. I'm not being mean. It's the truth. It's not your fault, but you don't know how much you don't know. It's called the hubris of youth," I explained.

In the darkness, the ghost glowered at me, her eyelids heavy and the corners of her mouth reaching for a frown. "I'm not *young*," she said. "Don't you remember the first time we met? You were little, and so was I. I've been on this earth every bit as long as you have."

I opened my mouth to object, but she had me there. After all, she didn't say she'd been *alive* as long as I had. "Fine, but as a ghost, you don't understand how people operate. Especially adults. You don't know why Andromeda says she wants to help. Maybe she really does. Maybe there's goodness in her heart, and she just wants to reconnect me with my past. It's possible."

"It's *more* than possible," the ghost said. "Andromeda has pink hair. Ladies with pink hair can't be bad."

"It's also possible she has a book deal in the works, and she's using me for a story no one else can tell," I said, ignoring her comment about pink hair. That didn't even warrant discussion. "Maybe it's something bigger than a book deal. Maybe it's a movie. Maybe it's a new television series. The point is, I can't read minds. I don't know what Andromeda wants. Maybe she wants to help me. Maybe she wants to help herself."

The ghost threw up her hands in exasperation. "Who cares? Don't you want to know what happened to those people? Don't you want to know where you came from?"

It took me a long time to answer. But finally, I shook my head. "Not really. I know you don't understand that. No one does. I just don't see the point in digging up the past. What good will it do?"

The ghost blinked. "What *harm* can it do?"

"I don't know, and that's the problem. I'm happy with my life. Why would I want to look for trouble?"

The ghost was quiet for a long time. Then she said, "Are you?"

"Am I what?"

"Happy," she said with a roll of her eyes, as if this were the most obvious thing in the world. "Are you happy?"

I sighed. "I don't know. Maybe. I think so. Or at least, I'm getting there."

The ghost smiled and leaned her head to the side. "I'm glad. You deserve to be happy."

"Do I?" I asked. "Sometimes, I wonder."

The ghost nodded. "I know. And that's the real reason you won't let Andromeda or anyone help you. Because you're not sure you deserve it."

"All right," I groaned. "Let's just do this, okay?"

The ghost frowned. "Do what?"

I retrieved my phone and began a Google search. I typed in the phrase, "Some of all profits +album". Google returned a bunch of links for fundraisers saying things like, "A portion of all profits will be donated..." or "Some of all profits will go toward funding..." so I nixed that search and tried another, this time adding "-fundraiser" to my search string. That didn't yield anything, either. I varied my search terms, looking for anything to point me in the right direction. But nothing turned up.

"There, I did my due diligence," I said, putting the phone away. "I searched for an album called *Some of All Profits,* and I didn't find anything. Are you happy?"

The ghost rolled her eyes. "This isn't about making *me* happy. Geez."

I yawned and glanced at the clock. It was getting late. I reached to my bedside table to turn off the lamp. "Well, I did it to shut you up, anyway. The truth is —"

But when I looked back over to where the ghost had been sitting, she was gone.

---

I woke up to the smell of muffins.

I wasn't especially hungry, but the smell coming from downstairs made my mouth water. I dressed quickly, ran a brush through my hair, and headed downstairs. I found Gluttony in the kitchen, pulling a tray of fresh blueberry muffins from the oven. A second batch was already cooling on the counter.

I slid onto a stool at the island and plopped my chin

in my hands. "You're up early," I said. "Couldn't sleep?"

Gluttony huffed and slid the muffins onto the counter. "That pan's hot." He untied the apron at his waist and hung it on a peg by the pantry. He ran a hand over his afro and huffed out a sigh. "I slept fine. Had to get up early to get a jump start on the day, though. Sloth and I have a lot to do, and she hasn't been herself lately. I thought these muffins might help."

"Not herself how?"

Gluttony grimaced and pulled a cooling rack from underneath the sink. "She's depressed," he said, using his fingertips to lift the hot muffins from the tray and drop them onto the rack. "And depressed people can't solve mysteries."

The muffins smelled terrific, and I reached for one, but Gluttony smacked my hand away. "Those are for Sloth."

I scowled but withdrew my hand into my lap. "I hate to break this to you, but she's always depressed. That's kind of why she's here. As a sin, I mean. Sloth doesn't just mean laziness like most people think. It has more to do with a general ennui of the soul."

Gluttony tilted his head back and barked out a laugh, placing a hand on each hip and standing akimbo. "I know you're not about to school me about the Bible," he said. "I been going to Sunday school since I was knee high to a grasshopper, and two of my uncles are ministers. I know what sloth means."

He picked up the now-empty tray with a pair of mitts and dropped it into the sink. "It's gotta be tough being a mind reader," he said. "I think she been hearing things lately she rather not hear. Things ain't goin' good for her, and I worry. And that ain't selfish. I mean, yes, I want to win this challenge, but I also care about the girl. Don't you tell nobody I said that." He jabbed an index finger at my face. "I'll just deny it."

Just then, Wrath bounded into the kitchen, a pair of headphones around his neck. As usual, he was dressed like something out of a cyberpunk comic, with an over-sized black T-shirt reaching almost down to his knees and a pair of polyester cargo pants with way too many zippers. "Hey," he said, slapping me on the arm. "You busy today?"

"Not especially," I said. "Why, you got a lead or something?"

Wrath smiled and lifted his hands, jabbing his thumbs toward his chest. "Who's got two thumbs and an appointment to talk to Victoria Webster?"

I spread my hands, supplicant. "Is this a riddle?"

"This guy," he said, breaking into a smile.

I sat up straight, blinking back my surprise. "Really? You got us an appointment with Victoria Webster? Why did you do that?"

"Well, you didn't *ask* for my help," Wrath said, his voice taking on an accusing tone. "But since that shaman didn't know squat about poltergeists, I figured maybe Victoria Webster would."

I spun around on the stool, still eyeing the muffins. "Yeah, definitely, but I thought it was more important to stay focused on the case. I'm afraid the poltergeists might be a dead end," I said.

Wrath pointed to the muffins. "Can I have one of

these?"

Gluttony glanced at Wrath. "No."

"Anyway," my partner said, sliding his headset up onto his ears, "if talking to Victoria helps us understand Jeff better, I'm all for it. Only problem is, she doesn't have time to see us in private. She agreed to meet us while she's getting her hair done."

I shrugged. If she was willing to talk, I was ready to listen. I didn't need privacy for an interview. "That's awesome, Wrath, thanks. What time's the appointment?"

He looked down at his smartwatch. "10 minutes ago," he said. "Let's bounce."

Incredulous, I stared after Wrath as he slipped from the kitchen. I turned to Gluttony, brow raised. "Can you believe that guy?"

Without waiting for an answer, I plucked a muffin from the island. The pastry was halfway to my mouth when Gluttony shouted, "Yo! Those are for Sloth!"

I bit into the muffin, and hot blueberry juice squirted over my tongue. "She won't mind. Tell her I said thanks," I said through a mouthful of blueberry juice and sugar.

Gluttony said nothing as he watched me devour the rest of the muffin. Then he smiled and tossed a rag onto his shoulder. "Have a great day, Pride."

Something about the way he said it stopped me in my tracks. "Gluttony? Wait! Did you—what did you put in the muffins? Gluttony?"

Gluttony tsked as he walked away. "I told you they were for Sloth. Next time, mind your manners."

# eight

. . .

The Beachin' Blondes hair salon was a quick 5-minute drive from the house. The entire time, I scolded Wrath for our lateness. "It's just so rude and unprofessional," I said, shaking my fists in the air for emphasis. "You of all people should understand that! You're so invested in social justice and everything."

Wrath gripped the wheel so hard, his knuckles went bloodless. "You think punctuality is on the side of the little guy? Oh man, you've got some serious deprogramming to do," he said, not waiting for my answer. "Let me tell you about *time* discipline, man. It cheats laborers out of optimizing their labor based on their natural rhythms, for one."

I pressed a hand to my forehead, closing my eyes as I leaned back into the seat. "You've got to be kidding me," I moaned.

"Think about it, Pride. Clock-time is what allowed the industrial revolution to be successful, man. Forcing people to work on the company's schedule instead of their own natural rhythms? That's what breaks people down. You think everyone in the working world wants to wake up at 6 a.m., work 8 or 9 hours, and then get in bed by 10? Our society shows no respect for different circadian rhythms, man. It's unjust."

"Why did I say anything?" I muttered to myself.

"And that's not all," he continued. "Time discipline and punctuality are tools of white supremacy."

I held up a hand. "I'll take your word for it," I said.

"Showing up late is an act of anarchy," Wrath said, ignoring me. "When we show up late to places? Especially appointments with rich ladies with more dollars than sense? We're sticking it to the man, you know? We're taking back our value."

As usual, Wrath's view of the world was too ridiculous to respond to. And anyway, the longer we drove, the less I felt inclined to change his mind. In fact, I was in a good mood. I felt lighter. My mind was clear, and negativity seemed to melt off me.

That was new to me. I kinda liked it.

The salon was exactly what you'd expect of a salon called Beachin' Blondes. It was decorated in the local beachy style, which I'm sure the city council appreciated. Most of the guests sported a head full of artificially blonde hair. The shades of blonde ranged from dark and sultry to silver so rich, it was almost purple. Bubblegum pop played from the speakers overhead, and as soon as we walked in, a woman draped in a black cape with her head full of foil lifted a hand.

"Wrath? Pride? Over here," she said.

The cameramen followed us over to Victoria's chair.

We'd brought two cameramen today. I say we brought them like we had a choice, which we didn't. But judging by the look on Victoria's face, two cameras were better than one.

One thing I've learned in my time in Odyssey? Everybody in this town has their sights set on stardom. Which, I won't lie, makes getting them to talk to us on camera easier.

"Nice to see you again, Victoria," Wrath said, turning on the charm.

Victoria smiled, flashing artificially white and even teeth. "I'd offer my hand, but this cape just gets in the way," she tittered. "Good to see you, too, Pride."

"Great to see you, too, Victoria. I have to say, you look just as lovely underneath that cape as you did the other night at the séance."

As soon as the words were out of my mouth, I blinked in shock. Why on earth had I said that? That wasn't anything I'd usually say. It wasn't even anything I'd typically think. Even Wrath was looking at me like I'd lost my mind. But I just shook myself and smiled, covering my bemusement. "So did Wrath tell you what we wanted to talk about today?"

Instead of answering, however, Victoria looked to her stylist and gestured toward a couple of empty chairs in the waiting area. "Shelley, would you mind bringing those chairs over here for our guests? We have so much to talk about, and I think they'd be more comfortable if they weren't on their feet the whole time."

Shelley hurried away to carry out the request, and Victoria rolled her eyes, making a disgusted sound behind the other woman's back. "Seriously, you'd think she would've known to do that on her own. Sometimes, it's just impossible to get good help."

When Shelley returned with the chairs, I clapped her on the arm, giving her shoulder a gentle squeeze. "I really appreciate this," I said, surprising even myself. "You really didn't have to do that."

Shelley's cheeks turned from pink to bright red as she fluttered her lashes, chewing her lips with what I think was embarrassment. "It's not a problem," she breathed, returning her attention to Victoria's head full of foiled hair.

"Anyway," Wrath said, settling into his chair, "we want to talk about Jeff."

Victoria nodded sagely. "Jeff Bishop," she cooed. She said his name like she was uttering a prayer. "It was such a travesty, the way he died. But at least he went out the same way he lived his life, right? With gusto. Doing the thing he loved."

I quirked an eyebrow. "Did Jeff love climbing?"

"It wasn't about the climbing," Victoria assured me. "It was all about conquering. Doing things the average person couldn't do. Jeff was not content with ordinary. How do you think he ended up with a woman like Tamora? Anyway, not everybody gets to die on top of Mount Everest. That's my point. Jeff was different. Right from the start."

I cleared my throat and leaned forward, lowering my voice. "Did you know him well? Did he confide in you?"

Now, the woman's eyes narrowed ever so slightly, and I caught a glance from the stylist in the mirror. "I don't know if I would call myself a confidante," she said. "We were close, though. I've known Jeff for a long time."

"How long?" Wrath asked.

"That's too close to asking a lady how old she is," Victoria said, dropping us a coy wink. "But I've known him since college. No, not like that." Victoria was glaring in the mirror at her stylist, pointing to a section of foils around her face. "I want these highlights to be thinner. You can't use such chunky sections."

"Sorry," Shelley apologized, removing the foils from her client's hair. "I wasn't thinking."

As she rearranged the foils, my eyes trailed up the stylist's bare arms. She had an array of artwork on her skin done in bright colors and bold lines. "Your tattoos are beautiful," I said. "Did you get that work done here?"

"Not in Odyssey," she said. "I had to go all the way to Toronto for these."

"It was worth it," I purred, still admiring her art. "Do they have special meaning for you?"

Even as I asked the questions, I had no idea why these words were coming out of my mouth. Not because her tattoos weren't lovely—they were—but because giving out compliments like Halloween candy was so far outside my comfort zone that I'd need a GPS to find my way back. And yet, I couldn't stop. "You have a real sense of style," I continued. "Do you do your own hair? The color is outstanding."

The stylist flushed red and touched her hair absently. "I do the color myself," she said, eyes glowing. "I change it too often to let anyone else do it. The expense would be outrageous." She chuckled, the color creeping higher into her face. "Someone else cuts it, though. It's really hard to cut your own hair."

"Well, whoever does it does a great job. The way it frames your face is just perfect."

Shelley sucked in a breath and dropped her eyes, but that smile lingered on her lips.

Suddenly, I felt Wrath's hand close around my upper arm, and he stepped away, dragging me along with him. "We'll be back in just a second," he said to Victoria.

Wrath's grip tightened as he pulled me across the salon and into a quiet corner. When we were out of earshot, Wrath practically threw my arm down. "What are you *doing*?" he demanded. "Why are you blathering on with the stylist? Are you trying to get her digits or something? I thought you had a thing for Lust!"

I wrapped both my hands around my throat and shook my head, my eyes wide. "First of all, nothing is going on between me and Lust. But second, I don't know what's happening! I can't help it! My brain is absolutely overflowing with positive thoughts! Like right now, I'm trying really hard not to tell you what nice hands you have. Your fingers are elegantly shaped, and your skin is so soft."

Wrath grabbed me by the shoulders, digging his fingertips into my skin as he gave me a good, hard shake. "Get it together, man! That rich lady's not gonna talk to us if she thinks we're lunatics."

"I'm trying," I whined. "But I feel like I've been drugged or something."

Wrath released me, arms falling limply to his sides. His mouth formed a soft *o*, and he let his eyes flutter closed as his head tipped backward. "You ate Gluttony's muffins," he said.

"He put something in them," I said, realizing it was true. "Some kind of magic to make people have nice thoughts. Probably so Sloth wouldn't have to hear everyone's internal garbage for just one day."

Wrath slapped me on the shoulder. "You gotta be careful what you stuff into your piehole, man! We're trying to win this thing. What if he'd put in magic to sabotage us?"

I frowned, shaking my head. "Gluttony wouldn't do that."

"That's not the point. You need to be more careful." He jerked his head back toward Shelley's station. "Okay, so, we're gonna go back over there, and I need you to *stay on target*. Focus on your questions, okay? Leave the stylist alone."

I tried to respond, but Wrath was already tugging me back across the salon. Victoria's face was pinched, and even I could tell she was growing irritated.

"Sorry about that," Wrath said. "We don't want to take up too much more of your time. But Pride had one question." He held out his hand, gesturing for me to speak.

"Right. One question," I said, trying hard to focus. It was harder than you think. All I could think about was how Victoria had nicely shaped eyes and a perfect nose and how Shelley's neck was the perfect length for her body. "Victoria, did Jeff ever mention poltergeists to you?"

Victoria's head snapped up, and her eyes met mine in the mirror. Her gaze was icy cold, her face frozen. But the expression was fleeting; as quickly as it had appeared, the ice melted, and her carefree aloofness returned with a cavalier smirk. "Poltergeists? You mean invisible ghosts that throw things around and scream in the middle of the night?"

I sucked in a sharp breath. This town seriously needed re-education about the supernatural. "Well, technically, poltergeists are not—"

"Yes," Wrath interrupted. "Exactly. Did he ever mention anything like that to you?"

Victoria shook her head. "No. Like I said, Jeff was very down to earth. Something like that would never come up in conversation."

But as she said it, her eye twitched.

I watched her in the mirror, waiting for her to change her tune, but she just stared back at me, not even blinking. "Okay," I said finally. It didn't look like she was gonna talk. But I couldn't ignore that twitching eye. She was definitely holding something back. "Listen. We're going to catch this person who's pretending to be Jeff," I said. "But to do that, we need to ask him questions— things only Jeff would know. Do you have anything? Something we could ask that maybe only you and Jeff shared?"

Victoria's mouth twisted, and her eyes listed toward the ceiling as she considered my question. But finally, she let her breath out in a controlled exhale. "I can't think of anything off the bat," she said. "If you're asking me for secrets—I'm sure I told him secrets over the years. But I couldn't tell you what they were about. And as for him sharing secrets with me? That wasn't really how Jeff operated."

I turned my attention back to Wrath. "I can't think of anything else," I said. "You?"

Wrath shook his head. "Nothing from me. But listen, Victoria. If you think of anything, would you call us?"

Victoria flashed us another of her bright smiles. "Of course! I'd do anything to help Tamora."

We were halfway to the car when a voice called out behind us.

"Wait."

We turned around to find Shelley hurrying over to us, her eyes darting around wildly, checking over her shoulder as though she was worried about being followed. She sidled up next to us, holding her hands at her chest. She twisted her fingers together and chewed on her bottom lip. "Can I talk to you for a second? In private?"

I shrugged, looking around. "You're talking to us in private right now."

Shelley swallowed hard a couple times, nodding. But she wasn't really agreeing. It was more like she was building up courage or convincing herself of something. After a little while, she said, "I don't have a lot of time, but Victoria's lying to you."

"Lying?" Wrath repeated.

Shelley smoothed her hair behind her ears (even though she already looked perfect) and continued to scan the parking lot for eavesdroppers. "I've been her stylist for a long time. She doesn't trust anybody else to make her blonde but me. And you know what they say about stylists and their customers? When people sit in that chair for a long enough time, they talk. They talk about all *kinds* of things."

I nodded, rolling my hand in a get-on-with-it motion. "Okay. What did she tell you?"

"I wouldn't feel right telling you everything," she began, "so I'll just tell you this. The Topanga Canyon Music Awards. They were only hosted for one year before they were canceled. Jeff was there, and he had a guest."

"A guest?"

But Shelley was already backing away, holding her hands out to ward off more questions. "Just look into it," she said. "I think it'll be worth your time."

Before we could ask her any more questions, she turned on her heel and ran back into the salon.

Wrath whistled as he watched her hurry back inside. "That was weird, right? Why didn't she just tell us what she knew?"

"No telling," I said, studying Wrath's profile. "You have a really nice jawline."

Wrath's cheeks burned pink, and he rolled his eyes, jamming a thumb toward the car. "Stop flirting with me and get in. Man, I hope that stupid muffin wears off sooner than later."

But he wasn't exactly frowning as he said it.

# nine

. . .

I slept until noon the next day. I could easily have slept longer, but sometimes, my housemates were the most inconsiderate people on earth. Someone was banging on a wall, and someone else—or maybe the same person, who knew?—was shrieking with laughter. Music was playing somewhere in the house, just loud enough to hear but not loud enough to make out what it was.

Grumbling, I pulled the covers over my head, foolishly hoping for a little more shut-eye. I was desperate to remain asleep, to ward off getting out of my cozy bed and dealing with cameramen just a little while longer. But then I smelled coffee and my body betrayed me, choosing the warm, steaming seduction of caffeine over another sixty minutes of dreamland.

Cursing under my breath, I climbed out of bed and pulled on a pair of sweatpants, an oversized t-shirt with glittery cupcakes on the front, and stuck my feet into a pair of slippers I'd inherited from Envy—fuzzy hedgehogs with pointy noses and whiskers and everything. How could you not want them?

I pulled a comb through my hair and went downstairs.

I found Lust in the kitchen. As usual, she looked great. Her long, dark hair was pulled away from her face in a high ponytail, which made her cheekbones look like they could cut glass. She wasn't wearing any makeup, and still she looked like America's Next Top Model. She was wearing a black Metallica t-shirt and cut-off shorts with the pockets peeking out of the bottom. I immediately regretted not putting on real clothes. But at least my loungewear was clean.

Lust took one look at me and turned to the coffeemaker, pouring me a fresh mug she shoved into my hands. "You look awful," she said, nose wrinkled. "Rough night?"

I wrapped my hands around the mug and took a deep breath of the steaming brew. I didn't know why Lust had a fresh pot of coffee on at 12 o'clock in the afternoon, but I sure was grateful for it. "Just couldn't sleep is all," I said, blowing across the top of my drink. "I keep thinking about poltergeists and dead guys and missing communes. It's just a lot."

Lust nodded and wound her ponytail into a bun. "I bet it is. If I had a vision of poltergeists like you did, I don't think I'd sleep for a week."

"Well, I've seen worse," I said. I tried to sip the coffee, but it was too hot. Luckily, just holding it made me feel better. "When I was still consulting for the police department, I once touched a guy and saw him murdering his own wife. And I saw it from his perspective, too, since that's how my gift—if you can call it that —works. I didn't want to touch anyone for months, and sleep was pretty much out of the question."

Lust's face paled, and I immediately realized my mistake. This was too heavy for morning conversation. Even though it wasn't technically morning. "Anyway, I don't want to talk about this right now."

Lust recovered quickly, pushing herself away from the counter and flashing me a bright smile. "Great! I don't want to talk about it, either. Anyway, listen. I'm glad you're awake. I was wondering if you wanted to accompany me into town."

"We are in town," I ventured cautiously. "This is town. Or did you mean another town?"

Lust shimmied up to me and wrapped her arms around my waist. I was so caught off-guard, I sloshed my coffee over the rim of the mug as I tried to maneuver the cup out from between us. With her hands clasped at the small of my back, she pulled herself right against me, giggling as I squirmed. I tried to wiggle free, but she was having none of it, pulling me closer the more I wriggled.

Not that I was wriggling *too* hard.

"I mean this town," she said with a laugh. She pressed her lips to my cheek in a quick peck and then let me go. She stepped away from me just as quickly as she'd moved in. "So what do you say? You up for it?"

The coffee was just cool enough to drink, so I closed my eyes and took a sip. Warmth flooded through my body, and the knots in my back and shoulders slowly gave up the ghost. "Getting out of the house would be good for me," I said at last. "Give me 20 minutes to get ready."

"You have 10," she said, bouncing away. "Don't be late!"

And before I could object, she disappeared around the corner.

———

"City-wide garage sale?"

We were walking toward the Cameron Events Center, merging with the throngs of bargain hunters who had come from miles around to rummage through castoff junk other people didn't want. Children in flip-flops with grubby faces squealed as they ran past me. Teenagers too cool for school meandered away from their parents, bumping shoulders playfully as they snickered and gossiped behind their hands. I turned to Lust, giving her my best "Are-you-serious?" look.

"What's this all about?"

Lust laughed as she linked her arm in mine and dragged me toward the entrance. She fished two 5-dollar bills from her pocket and turned them over to an attendant who stamped our hands and welcomed us inside. A frigid blast of conditioned air ruffled my hair as I stepped through the door.

"Shopping!" she exclaimed, spinning in a circle with her arms flung out at her sides. "I haven't been to a real, live flea market in something like fifteen years. I used to go all the time when I was a kid. When I heard this was happening, I couldn't get here fast enough."

I looked around, taking it all in. I'd heard of flea markets before, of course, but I'd never actually been to one for several reasons:

1. I hated shopping.
2. While I'd heard the aphorism "One man's trash is another man's treasure," I had not found this to be true.
3. Flea markets seemed like something old people did.
4. I hated shopping.

"Where should we start?" Lust asked, already tugging me toward a display of taxidermy alligator heads. Why any person would have an entire collection of stuffed alligator heads was beyond me. She picked up the smallest one and thrust it in my face. It had pointy teeth and marbles for eyes. "What do you think of this?"

"What are we doing here?" I asked, shoving the alligator aside. "I know you didn't bring me all the way out here to help you select Halloween décor."

Frowning, Lust set the alligator head aside and moved on to a display of insects cast in resin. "I want to get a gift for Gluttony. He's been taking *very* good care of Sloth, and I want him to know someone noticed."

"That's nice of you," I said, wondering if buying gifts for people showing minimal displays of courteousness was common. Nobody had ever given me a gift for having basic human decency. But maybe baking Happy

Thoughts muffins for depressed mind readers was above and beyond. I had no idea. What passed for normal social behavior continued to mystify me. To hide my confusion, I picked up a giant African beetle and looked for the price tag. When I found it, I put it back down.

People wanted way too much money for their worthless junk.

"Do you think he'd want an alligator head or some insects?" I asked, eyeing the rest of the wares at the booth with skepticism. "He doesn't strike me as the type."

"Well, he's from Louisiana," Lust explained. "So."

"Just because he's from Louisiana—look. I have a better idea." I grabbed her by the hand and led her away from the taxidermy animals, past some vintage photographs of other people's families, and past a huge collection of eyelet pillowcases. When I found what I was looking for, I stopped.

"He'll like this much more," I said.

Lust's eyes grew wide as she took in the vintage copper bakeware. Rooster-shaped cake pans, bread pans shaped like squash, and various Jell-O molds shaped like fish covered two folding tables. "You know you're an absolute genius?" She selected a muffin tin, examined it, and set it aside. "I don't know why I didn't think of this. Well, yes I do," she said, heaving out a sigh. "We're stumped on our case, and it's really getting to me. When you and I worked together, I felt like everything just gelled, you know? But this feels like work."

I nodded, rifling through the bakeware just to give my hands something to do. I had no interest in used cooking utensils. Frankly, the idea gave me the willies. Which doesn't make sense if you think about it. Eating at a restaurant is no different from eating from a stranger's kitchen. But at least restaurants have health inspectors. I'd seen too many pictures online of cats sitting in mixing bowls to believe most people's kitchens were anyplace I'd ever want to dine.

Lust chose a bundt pan shaped like a sandcastle. "What do you think of this one?" She held it with both hands against her chest.

"Looks impractical," I said.

She turned to the old man manning the booth. "I'll take it."

With Gluttony's present secured, I assumed we were done. But as Lust looped her arm through mine and began slowly meandering through the crowds, I realized I was wrong. We had ambled maybe fifty feet when she squealed in my ear and dashed toward a booth.

"Won't you *look* at these," Lust cooed. We were standing at a booth selling antique dolls of all shapes and sizes. "How *cute* are these?"

"Not cute at all," I said, my brow scrunched in a frown. "Old dolls are creepy. That you like them is weird."

Lust chuckled, tilting her face to meet my gaze. "Why is it weird that I like them?"

I swept my hand vaguely along the vertical lines of her body. "Because in some ways, you're so normal. Like, profoundly normal. Like Miss America poster girl normal. And then you go and say stuff like how you're into creepy dolls."

Lust selected a doll wearing a red velvet dress with white fur on the collar and cuffs. If you'd told me the doll was supposed to be Mrs. Claus as a weird baby, I would have believed you. "And in other ways, I'm as abnormal as they come," she reminded me, running the velvet between her fingers. "That's how I ended up on the show. Well, that and a completely broken sense of self-esteem."

It was hard to tell whether this was a topic Lust wanted to talk about or not, so I said nothing, letting her lead the way. She replaced the doll she was holding and chose another. This one was African and draped in traditional Kente cloth. "When Tricia first presented the idea of living with a bunch of strangers, I was completely put off. To be honest, I thought it was the most ridiculous thing I'd ever heard. I had a good job, and I was happy. I wasn't in a committed relationship, so that wasn't ideal, but everything else in my life was going fine. So why would I want to move to California into a beach house and live with a bunch of strangers?"

"The grand prize," I answered. "You wanted to win your heart's desire like everyone else."

"That's true," she drawled, the corner of her mouth dripping into a frown. "But there was more to it than that."

She hesitated, her bottom lip folded beneath her teeth. Her eyes darted aimlessly, like she was debating whether to tell me something. Finally, she looked away and said, almost offhandedly, "It also felt like fate. Do you know what I mean?"

I was quiet a beat too long, and Lust laughed

nervously, shaking her head. "No, look. I mean, I get it. They wanted psychics in the house. And there's probably not a ton of real psychics out there. Certainly not a ton of psychics with my particular personality flaws." She reached for her hair. Lust usually wound a lock of hair around her finger when she was nervous, but with her hair in a bun, she had little to play with. Instead, she stroked absently at the baby hair at her temple. "But in a way, that confirms my point. I felt like I was made for this role. And I know it's not a role. I mean, I know it's real life. Sort of." She blew out her frustration in a noisy raspberry. "Gah. I don't know what I'm trying to say."

We were walking again. I didn't know what Lust was trying to say, either, but I got the feeling she just needed to talk. So I made encouraging noises and slowed my pace to match hers. "I guess what I'm saying is, it wasn't a rational thought that led me to the show. It was more like a guiding hand. Something I needed that I didn't even know about."

I was about to respond that I didn't believe in fate when Lust shrieked.

We had just wandered to a booth selling a large variety of tiaras—silver ones, gold ones, metal ones, plastic ones. She thrust the bag with Gluttony's present into my chest. Then she darted to the table, immediately choosing a silver tiara with several tiers of glittering rhinestones. Gingerly, she placed it on top of her head, examining herself in the provided mirror.

I cringed. Not because Lust looked bad—that was impossible—but because knowing countless other people may have tried on that accessory gave me the willies.

What if somebody had lice? Could you get lice from trying on a tiara?

Luckily, I schooled my face into a more neutral position before Lust turned to me, expectant. "Does this work?" She placed both hands on her hips and turned in a slow circle so I could admire her from every angle. The fake jewels atop her head sparkled in the overhead fluorescent lights. She looked ridiculous, but not in a bad way. But you can't tell someone they look ridiculous without them taking it the wrong way. So instead, I said, "Excellent. You look excellent."

Gently, she removed the tiara and placed it on the table, pawing through the other options. "I've always wanted one of these," she confessed. "I feel like this is a sign. The universe wants me to have a tiara."

I wasn't sure why a table full of tiaras was a sign from the universe while a table full of taxidermy beetles wasn't. Still, I wasn't in any position to argue. Instead, I tucked Gluttony's gift under my arm and helped Lust sort through the tangle of headwear. I found one tiara that reminded me of Lust. It was more ornate than the others, but also elegant. "What do you think of this one?"

Lust lifted the tiara from my hands and placed it daintily atop her head. She peered down into the mirror, her face lighting up like candles on a birthday cake. "It's gorgeous," she breathed. She straightened up, her lips twisting into a smile as color rose into her cheeks. "Can I tell you something? Promise not to tell anyone ever."

I drew an X over my chest. "Cross my heart," I said.

Lust raised an eyebrow. "And hope to die?"

I hesitated. "No?"

My housemate stepped closer to me and lowered her voice. "Years ago, there was this website called Like It or Leave It. It was basically a vanity site for dumb girls like me who were insecure about their looks. You posted pictures of yourself, and complete strangers voted on how much they'd like to date you. You had to register, so it wasn't like any troll could randomly drive by and drop you a 1 out of 10. Well, I was so insecure that I posted my very best picture, and after a week or so, my average was something like a five."

I didn't say anything, but if she was only getting a five, the site was definitely full of trolls, required registration or not. But I kept that to myself.

"Anyway, to make myself feel better, I made a fake account. Actually, I made multiple fake accounts. Then I logged into my main account and added my fake accounts as my friends. You know, to give them the look of legitimacy. I know it's stupid," she said. "That's how desperate I was. I voted for myself with my various fake accounts. I left messages to myself and everything." She rolled her eyes, removing the tiara from her head and gazing down at it lovingly. "I figured if it looked like I was desirable to others, I would *become* desirable to others. I know that's pathetic, but in some ways, I'm still that girl," she said. "Still looking for validation. Still…" She looked up at me and made a face. "What is it? What are you thinking?"

I hadn't even realized I wasn't fully listening to Lust until she called me on it. But what she just said about making fake accounts and friending them sent bolts of lightning down my spine. I pressed a hand to my forehead as realization dawned. "*That's* how I'll find him," I said aloud, but primarily to myself. "Why didn't I think of this sooner?"

Lust narrowed her eyes and tilted her head to the side. "Find who?"

"The real identity of Cecil Bradshaw," I said. "I just realized—"

"Are you thinking about your case?" Lust gave me a long blink and a slight shake of her head. "I'm pouring my heart out to you—revealing my deepest vulnerabilities—and you're thinking about your *case?*"

I took the tiara from Lust's hands and gave it to the woman behind the booth. "I'll take this one," I said. Then I turned back to Lust. "Do you remember why my girlfriend left me?"

Lust's face softened, but only a little. "Yes. You missed her sister's wedding."

"That was the final straw," I agreed, "but it wasn't the real problem. The real problem was that I have attention deficit. I get hyper-focused on work, and I lose track of everything else. Lots of times, I didn't even come home. I slept in my car or at the office. It never occurred to me that Shayda was expecting me. I wasn't thinking about her at all."

Lust's nostrils flared. "I suppose you're telling me this so I'll feel sorry for you?"

"I'm telling you this because you can't take it personally," I said. The salesclerk returned the tiara wrapped in a bag, and I handed it to Lust. "This is who I am. You're a siren who flirts too much. I'm a forgetful, attention-challenged moron with no feel for relationships."

She looked down at the package in her hands. "Is that why you bought me the tiara? To make up for your shortcomings?"

I shook my head. "No. I bought it because you liked it, so I wanted you to have it. That's all."

Without warning, Lust pulled me into an embrace and whispered, "Thanks, Pride. That really means a lot to me."

"You're welcome," I said, wriggling free of her arms.

The truth was, it meant a lot to me, too. But unfortunately for both of us, I could never, ever admit it.

———

When I got back to Sinful House, I barged into Wrath's room without knocking. He was sitting at his computer, headphones on, lights out. He didn't turn around at my entry, so he must not have heard. I glanced at his monitor—he was playing a classic first-person shooter game. I snatched the headphones off his head and tossed them onto the desk.

Wrath spun around, fury and disbelief scrambling his features. "What the crap do you think you're doing, Pride? That was a championship PvP match! Do you know how bad that's gonna tank my rating?" He noticed the cameraman over my shoulder and regulated his tone. "This better be important."

"I have an idea how to figure out who Cecil Bradshaw is," I said.

A loud, annoyed sigh rattling in his throat, Wrath ran his hands through his hair, making it stand up in pale yellow spikes. "Man, this better be good. You're so gonna owe me otherwise."

"Go to Cecil's Facebook page," I instructed.

Wrath frowned as he swiveled around to face the monitor. He typed the URL into the browser. "We already *did* this, remember?"

"We did," I agreed, "but we didn't know what we were looking for. Now I do."

Cecil's page loaded up, replete with that ridiculous photograph of the Israeli model. I pointed to his friends list. "Click that," I said. "I want to go through all his friends. He doesn't have many, so it shouldn't take long."

Wrath clicked the link, still scowling. "And what are we looking for?"

"The real Cecil Bradshaw."

I quickly explained what Lust had told me about making fake accounts for herself and then friending them to give herself more legitimacy. "…So that got me thinking Cecil might have done the same thing. One of his 'friends' may actually be him."

"Not a terrible idea," Wrath said with grudging admiration. At least, I think it was admiration. It was hard to tell with Wrath. "You know, this'll go quicker if we both use our own computers."

I leaned down to whisper into his ear. "It'll look better for the cameras if we do it together."

He grunted but didn't argue. He clicked the first link.

"What *exactly* are we looking for?"

"I have no idea," I said, scanning the first friend's profile. "Something that stands out."

"What kind of something?"

I grimaced, hands dug deep in my pockets. "I don't know. Let's just see what we see."

The first profile was for a man named Linton Bonner. Linton was older, maybe mid-sixties, with salt and pepper hair and a lined, tanned face. His profile featured his wife and grown kids, even a grandchild. I shook my head. "This isn't him."

Wrath backtracked and clicked the next link. "Andy Garcia," Wrath read aloud. "Looks like he's the right age. Not that there's an age limit on scammers, but." We scrolled through his pictures. No sign that he was married. Most of his photos featured him wearing Civil War reenactment garb.

"Guys who play dress-up might fake being a medium," Wrath said after clicking through a dozen photos. "We like him for Cecil?"

"Maybe," I said, jotting his name down on a stray piece of paper. We couldn't rule him out, but it wasn't pinging my psychic senses, either. Not that I was an expert in this sort of thing.

The next profile was for Britni Newsome, who was dressed in scanty bikinis in every photo. Wrath clicked more of her photos than was necessary. After the fifth or sixth, I cleared my throat loudly. "This is definitely a fake account," I said. "Next."

We clicked through profiles, jotting down the names of anyone we couldn't rule out. More than half the profiles were private, but Wrath bypassed those limitations by sweet-talking the computer, a feat that I was learning to envy more each day.

We'd been at it for about forty-five minutes when Wrath froze, his mouse wheel stopping mid-spin.

"Whoa, Pride. Look."

We were looking at the profile of a man named Jace Thornburgh. According to his profile, he studied at Carnegie Mellon University, was from Little Rock, Arkansas, and now lived in San Francisco. He was the CEO of Triplex Virtual. He had no relationship status listed.

He was a good-looking man: late thirties, olive skin, tousled, dark hair, and bushy eyebrows. His profile picture showed him laughing, his face pressed alongside the slobbering muzzle of a Golden Retriever. He looked like your typical all-American guy.

And then I saw what Pride saw. "Click the thumbnail," I said. I was so excited, my voice had risen an octave.

The photograph loaded, and both Wrath and I stared in mute awe. Jace Thornburgh was dressed in a red Gore-Tex shell coat with a hood over a wool hat with built-in earmuffs. His face was red with cold, but he was smiling brightly.

Standing next to him, arms around his shoulders and face pressed close was a very familiar face.

"You've got to be kidding me," I breathed, leaning in for a closer look. "Is that…?"

"Jeff Bishop," Wrath confirmed. "The guy with Jace Thornburgh is Jeff Bishop. And look where they are."

Quickly, I read the caption. "Can't believe my luck.

Met my idol Jeff Bishop on this expedition. He was cool enough to take a selfie with me. I knew Mt. Everest would change my life. Little did I know it would save my career."

"Mount Everest," I said. "That's where Jeff died."

"Yeah." Wrath nodded, pointing to the date. "This photo was posted before his death."

I scanned the rest of the page, my heart thumping loudly in my ears. "But these comments weren't," I said. "At least, not all of them."

Here's what the original comments from Jace Thornburgh's friends said:

**Becca Caldwell:**

OMG! That's crazy! You are so lucky!

**Kyle Harabedian:**

My brother met him once. Said he was a super nice guy even in real life.

**Jace Thornburgh:**

He totally is. Very down to earth. We even talked about him potentially investing in DuGood (and saving it!!), and he told me to ping him once we were both back in the States!

**Albert Qian:**

Only you could use your last dollar to climb Everest to "find yourself," and then meet a crazy rich donor. Somebody upstairs must really like you.

**Jace Thornburgh:**

I know! When I told my business partner I was

doing this, he said I was out of my mind. He said no investor would touch us with a 10-foot pole if word got out I went bankrupt to climb a mountain. Rofl. Looks like I won't need them after all!

**Brandon Ward:**

Wow, cool!

**Jackie O'Neil:**

Awesome! You look great, by the way—very happy for you!

But then time elapsed, and the comments changed.

**Kyle Harabedian:**

Wondered if this photo was still here. So sad about his death. So glad you made it back down safe.

**Anne Preacher:**

I hope you got his autograph! You might be able to sell it and get the money he was gonna give you for your startup! LOL!

> **Brandon Ward:**
>
> WOW. That's the tackiest thing I've ever seen anyone post in public.

> **Anne Preacher:**
>
> Lighten up. It's not like he's gonna read this.

**Joey Barber:**

RIP Jeff Bishop.

**Anne Preacher**

RIP DuGood Virtual. 😭

"Wow, that Anne Preacher chick is a real jerk," Wrath said.

"Yeah, but thanks to her, I might have an idea." I tapped a finger against my lips, thinking. "Can you look up DuGood Virtual?"

Wrath navigated away from the page and googled the company. The first result was the website for the startup; we ignored that. The second result was a news story from Righteous Startup News. It was dated three weeks ago.

Wrath clicked it.

Here's what it said:

"Founded just two short years ago, DuGood Virtual was destined to change the world with its cutting-edge app. Early funding put the company on the map as a darling of Silicon Valley. In a sea of tech companies crowing that they would 'change the world,' DuGood Virtual was notable for actually attempting to do what others only gave lip service to.

"The technology connected underprivileged, third-world teenagers with venture capitalists who would mentor them and fund projects intended to eradicate poverty and education disparity in developing countries. However, the company today announced its dissolution. According to founder and CEO Jace Thornburgh, the company's finances were mismanaged, forcing them to shutter their endeavor when no other investors were willing to bet on Thornburgh's vision.

"But the world hasn't seen the last of Jace Thornburgh. While he wouldn't give details, the serial entrepreneur says he has another ace up his sleeve and a new company in the works. 'I'm just waiting for my funding to pan out,' Thornburgh says with a smile. 'Private donor. I can't really talk about it. But give me time. You haven't seen the last of Jace Harris Thornburgh.'"

Wrath swiveled around in his seat, facing me. His hair was still sticking up all over his head, which, paired with the maniacal grin, made him look like a villain from a children's cartoon. "So let me get this straight. Jace Thornburgh founds a tech company. But it's not going well, so he climbs a mountain to clear his head. While he's up there, he meets Jeff Bishop and hits him up for money. But Bishop dies before Thornburgh can get the money, and his company goes belly-up. So, then, what, he hatches a plan to marry Bishop's widow hoping to get the money he was promised?"

I rocked back onto my heels, my head swimming. I knew people were inherently selfish. But this seemed like a lot for someone wanting to change the world. "I hate to jump to conclusions, but yeah. Assuming Jace Thornburgh is the real Cecil Bradshaw, that's what this sounds like to me."

Wrath whooped, pumping his fists in the air as he leaped to his feet. "Did we just do it, Pride? Did we just *actually* solve this thing?"

I looked back to the monitor, the slightest smile breaking across my face. "It's too early to say for sure," I said. "Let's follow the trail wherever it leads."

Wrath clapped me on the shoulder, his smile so big, it threatened to crack his face in two. "Should we go tell Bailey? Should we go break the good news?"

"Yes," I said, my own smile broadening to match my housemate's. "Let's do it."

# ten

· · ·

At Bailey's house the next day, we shared everything we had learned about the case. We nestled in the couches in her sitting room and told her about the photos of the Israeli model and the strange visions about the poltergeists. We also told her about the women we'd messaged on Facebook, none of whom we'd heard back from yet. "We also looked up his phone number. It is registered to a guy named Cecil Bradshaw in San Francisco, so that's something. But we haven't called him yet."

Bailey's eyebrows shot high. "Why not? Seems like that would be the most logical thing to do."

"If we call him too early, we'll just spook him," Wrath said. "We were waiting until we had something on him. We wanted to ask him about something only Jeff would know. But so far, everyone we talked to says the same thing: Jeff was crazy private. They couldn't really think of anything notable Jeff shared with only them."

Bailey nodded, looking thoughtful. "Well, that's true. He was private. Still, you'd think *somebody* shared a moment with him, right? Maybe a funny inside joke between just the two of them? I mean, you can just make something up, can't you? Like, say, remember the time at Jenny's party when you got so drunk, blah blah blah, and if he says he remembers, you know it's a lie."

Wrath shook his head. "Only an idiot would fall for that. If I were pretending to be a dead guy, I'd pretend like I remembered almost nothing. It seems logical that a lot of your memories would go by the wayside after you kicked the bucket. We have to ask about something significant. Something you wouldn't forget, even in death."

"I see," Bailey said. "Well…I know you've been hard at work, and I don't mean to be rude, but it seems you haven't made that much progress at all."

Wrath and I exchanged looks. "Well," I drawled, "we haven't told you the best part yet."

Bailey's brows shot up. "Well, don't keep me waiting! What else did you find?"

Instead of telling her, I pulled up Jace Thornburgh's profile on Facebook and showed her the picture of him with Jeff. She read through the comments, her eyes wide, her hand pressed to her mouth. When she was done, she shook her head in amazement. "This is the guy, right? This has to be the guy."

"We think so, too," Wrath said. "But when we call and confront him, we want to really shatter his world. Hit him with all the evidence at once. So we're still following up on every lead. Which is where you come in."

Bailey leaned forward, intrigued. "Okay?"

"Victoria Webster's hairstylist said something weird," Wrath said. "She told us to look into the Topanga Canyon Music Awards. Do you know anything about that?"

Bailey tapped her fingers against her chin as she thought. "Vaguely. It was a cross between a music awards show and a fashion show. It was over 20 years ago, though. I was just a child. If I recall correctly, that show only happened once."

"That's right," I said. "Shelley—that's the stylist—said the same thing. She also said Jeff was there with a guest. You wouldn't know anything about that, would you?"

Bailey's mouth curved into a frown, and her shoulders sagged. "No, I'm sorry. I wasn't there. Dad went with Mom, and Tammy and I stayed home. But you know…" She pressed a hand to her cheek and looked up toward the ceiling. "I think there was a write-up in PopCharts Magazine about the awards show. Maybe there's something in there you can use."

"It's worth a look. Does the Odyssey library have archives? Micro-whatever?" Wrath asked.

Bailey grinned enthusiastically. "Microfiche. But anyway, you don't need the library! I still have most of Daddy's music stuff, including all the magazines he was in. It's all upstairs. Come with me. I'll show you."

We followed Bailey up the winding staircase and through the hallways until we came to an office. Or, more accurately, what used to be an office but had recently been ravaged by a tornado. The room was packed with junk—photographs, awards, papers, CDs, and more.

"Sorry about the mess," Bailey said, "but nobody uses this room. It's just where I keep Dad's stuff until I can figure out what to do with it." She pointed to a wall piled high with banker's boxes. "All of Dad's paper memorabilia is in there. If he still has a copy of PopCharts from the Topanga Canyon year, it'll be in there."

I gestured to the wall of boxes. "Any particular place the magazine is most likely to be?" I gulped as I took in the task before us. "This is a lot."

Bailey shook her head. "No, sorry. None of it's organized. At least, not that I'm aware of." She blew out a breath and stood up straight, squaring her shoulders. "Well, I guess I'll leave you to it. I hope you find what you're looking for. If you need anything, I'll just be downstairs."

As soon as Bailey was out of the room, Wrath took charge. He pointed to one end of the wall. "I'll start on this end," he said. "You start at that end, and we'll meet in the middle." Wrath whistled as he surveyed the mountain of boxes in front of us. "We've really got our work cut out for us." He turned to the camera crew. "Why don't one of you idiots put the stupid camera down and help us search?"

The camera guy shifted and snapped his gum. "We don't get paid to do nothing but work the camera. It's not in our International Cinematographers Guild contract."

Wrath blinked. "There's a guild for camera guys?" He turned to me, eyes wide. "Did you know there's a guild for camera guys?"

"Yes," I said, which was a lie, but I didn't need to admit my ignorance in front of the cameramen. Or the rest of America. "Wrath, forget about them. We have work to do."

"I'm just saying, man. I want a guild! There's no guild for reality show contestants. I asked my agent about it. She said we're not even covered by SAG because technically, we're not actors! We're supposed to *be ourselves*, whatever that means!" He kicked at a pile of books. "This is oppression, man! I feel exploited!"

I sighed. It was going to be a long day.

"Wrath, please just get to work."

He muttered one more thing about sticking it to the man before opening his first box.

It's surprising how much stuff a person can accumulate throughout their lives. And I'm talking about regular people, not even pack rats and stuff. As I sorted through the boxes looking for magazines with any reference to the Topanga Canyon Music Awards, I came across all kinds of things: letters from fans, signed photographs, sheet music, scratch paper with lyrics jotted down. I also found notebooks filled with random stuff: ideas, poems, shopping lists. It was like rifling through Adam Preston's mind.

It was unnerving.

"After I die, I hope all my stuff gets thrown away," I

said, flipping through what felt like my millionth magazine. "I don't want anybody pawing around my personal stuff. This is mortifying."

Wrath was holding a Playboy magazine at arm's length, rotating it so the centerfold fell out vertically. He looked at it for a minute, brows wriggling. Then he tossed it aside. "You won't care," he said, picking up another Playboy. "You'll be dead."

"Wrath." I pointed to the magazine. "Really?"

He made a disgusted face and tossed the magazine into a pile with the others. "What? A guy can't look?"

"No," I said. "Not when we're trying to stop a woman from marrying a shyster trying to take half her fortune."

"We don't know that for sure," Wrath said, digging through a fresh box. "He could be trying to take *all* her money."

Wrath was almost to the bottom of his box when he clapped his hands together and shouted in victory. "I think I found it!"

I dropped the magazine I'd been holding and walked over to where Wrath was flipping through an old, tattered copy of PopCharts. "I think this is it, man," he said. "There's a photo on the front page of the Topanga Canyon event. This has to be it. Please, *please* be something in here we can use."

He paged through the magazine until he came to the cover story. I leaned over his shoulder, trying to read the text, but Wrath was only looking at the pictures. He flipped through almost to the end of the article, which was long. With each page turn, I felt my heart sink a little more. If there was nothing in the article about Jeff Bishop's guest, we would have to track Shelley down and get her to talk. I wasn't sure that would be so successful.

But just when I was losing hope, Wrath stabbed the magazine with a finger. "That's it," he said. "Read this."

I leaned in to get a better look. Sure enough, the picture was a black-and-white image of Jeff Bishop's father, music producer Kerry Bishop. On Kerry's right was a younger version of Jeff. Even though he was a young teenager in the photo, he looked much the same. On Kerry's left was a young woman. She was gazing up at Kerry adoringly. Kerry's arms wrapped around both young people, and both he and Jeff were smiling brightly at the camera.

The caption underneath read, Kerry Bishop with son, Jeff, 15, and foster daughter, Tori Webb, age 13."

I pondered this for a minute. "This must've been what Shelley was talking about. Doesn't really seem like she's Jeff's guest, though. She's more—"

"His foster sister," Wrath said, snapping his fingers as a light bulb went off in his head. "Holy Godzilla, Pride. Take a closer look at that picture. Does that girl remind you of anyone?"

I studied the photo. Not only was it in black and white, which didn't help, but the young people in the picture were adults by now. And while Jeff looked recognizably the same, the woman could have been anyone.

"She doesn't look familiar," I said.

Wrath thumped the photo and made a popping sound with his lips. "Man, you need to get your eyes checked. Imagine this girl with blonde hair instead of brown and a smaller, straighter nose. Who does it look like?"

I examined the picture a moment longer, and then it hit me. "Victoria Webster?" I asked, incredulous.

Wrath was beaming. "That's her, man. That's Victoria Webster. Look. The girl in the photo is named Tori Webb. Tori Webb/Victoria Webster? It's the same girl."

I stared at Wrath, hardly even daring to blink. "Victoria Webster was Jeff Bishop's *foster sister?*"

Wrath grinned like a madman. "Looks like we gotta go talk to Vicki again. Somebody's got some 'splainin' to do."

---

"I don't owe you any explanation. Please, just leave me alone."

Thanks to Wrath's charm (?) and a very chatty assistant, we tracked Victoria down to the beach. She was walking her dog, an enormous and playful Labrador, as she kicked her way through the sand, arms folded petulantly across her chest.

I put a hand on her shoulder, but she yanked away, her stride quickening. "Victoria, please. I just want to understand. You said you met Jeff in college, but that's not true. You grew up with him. You two lived together in the same house."

She whirled on me, a finger pointed in my face. "Just because you saw an old photo in some stupid magazine doesn't mean—"

"When I touched you, I *saw* the poltergeists," I pressed on. "I told Tamora about the visions, and she said those were Jeff's memories. I didn't understand how I was seeing someone else's memories through a third party. But if you grew up with Jeff, it all makes sense. I didn't see Jeff's memories at all, did I? I saw yours."

Victoria shook her freshly blonde bangs away from her face. I couldn't see her eyes behind her massive black sunglasses, but I saw the taut pull of her lips as her mouth arced into a frown. "You had no right digging into my past," she said. "I didn't ask for that, and I don't want it. I want to help Tamora, too. But not if it costs me my privacy. Nothing is worth that."

"I understand," I said. "That night at the séance? I didn't know Tamora was going to ask Andromeda about the disappeared commune. I was angry about it. I don't want anyone digging into my past, either." I softened my voice, trying to make myself sound vulnerable. That was especially hard for me since *vulnerable* is the thing I try hardest not to be. "We're calling Cecil in the next few days. I need to prove he's not who he says he is. The only anecdote I have to use against him is the poltergeists. Please, Victoria. Help us out here."

Victoria stopped walking and turned her head towards the cameramen. "I won't say a word on camera," she said. "Not a single word. But get rid of them… and I'll talk."

Turning away, Wrath strode over to the camera crew. "Go on, get outta here," he said, shooing them off with grand, swooping arm gestures. "She's not gonna sign any release forms, so there's no point filming this. I'm serious. Get outta here!"

The cameramen walked backward, still filming. "Just let us get some B roll, man. We'll turn off the audio."

Wrath bent down and picked up a sand bucket and hurled it at the cameramen. He launched a second and a third, too. They each hit their targets squarely in the chest. "I'm not asking! Get outta here! You don't want to tick me off, man. I have no problem grabbing that camera and throwing it in the ocean. Just watch me."

That seemed to do the trick because the crew grumbled something and lowered the cameras to their sides. The red blinking lights went out. We watched them head back towards town, and only when we were sure they were out of earshot did Victoria relax a little.

"I moved in with the Bishops when I was nine," she began. "My mother was an alcoholic, and I was taken away from my family. My mother was supposed to regain custody once she got sober, but that never happened. I ended up living with the Bishops until I was 15." She sat down in the sand, and Wrath and I followed suit. Her dog was still running around, splashing and barking, tail wagging a mile a minute. Victoria watched him, a ghost of a smile playing across her face, but it quickly evaporated when she returned to the story. "You can't imagine what it's like to go from living in poverty to living with wealthy people. I can hardly tell you what my life was like. On the one hand, I felt blessed. The Bishops treated me well, and I had everything I wanted. On the other hand, I had terrible survivor's guilt. All the kids I grew up with, kids I knew from other homes? I knew they weren't doing half as well as I was. And I struggled with that. But before long, that survivor guilt stuff went away. And in a lot of ways, the guilt was better."

Victoria looked down at her hands, worrying the diamond rings on her fingers. "The first time I experienced the disturbances, I was alone. Jeff was in his room, and the Bishops were out. A book fell off a shelf in the middle of the night. I got up and replaced it. When I got back into bed, a second book fell. Then a third. That's when I got freaked out. My heart was pounding in my ears, but I couldn't let the books just lay on the floor. It felt disrespectful. So I climbed out of my blankets and put the books back on their shelves. When I got back into bed, I looked, and all the shelves were empty. Everything was on the floor."

She looked up and removed her sunglasses, revealing liquid eyes. "I was terrified. I pulled the blankets over my head and prayed for it all to end. Luckily, nothing else happened that night. Nothing else happened for several weeks. But then one night, Jeff and I were watching movies in his room. His closet door started banging open, shut. Open, shut."

Victoria wiped a tear with her fingers and cleared her throat. "They happened frequently after that. Dishes flying. Door slamming. Items falling off shelves. The disturbances only happened when Jeff's parents were out. We told them about it, but of course, they didn't believe us. And this was long ago, before everyone had a video camera in their pocket."

"How long did this go on?" Wrath asked.

Victoria shrugged. "Years. Until Jeff moved out for college. After he left, the disturbances stopped altogether. I never saw another dish fly off a shelf or another door slam in my face. But soon afterward, Mrs. Bishop died. Kerry either couldn't or didn't want to care for me after that. I got moved to a different foster home."

"That must've been hard for you," I said.

The freshly-blonde woman chortled. "You don't know the half of it."

"Did you keep in touch with the Bishops afterward?"

Victoria shook her head. "No. I never saw Kerry Bishop again. But one day, a lawyer called and asked me to come into his office. Jeff was there. We took one look at each other and burst into tears. His father had recently died, and Jeff inherited everything. He called me there because he said he owed me. I said he didn't owe me anything, but he insisted. And that day, Jeff signed over half his wealth to me. I became an instant millionaire. I used the opportunity to reinvent myself. I changed my name, my hair, my nose…I didn't need to be the trailer trash girl that grew up in foster homes anymore. I could be Victoria Webster. I could be someone."

"And you never told anyone about the poltergeists?" Wrath asked.

Victoria sneered. "Definitely not. Even Jeff and I never talked about it. We suffered through the disturbances, but after a certain age, we *never* spoke of them. Only Tamora knows. Well, and now the two of you."

We were quiet a while, nothing but the sound of the

surf rolling in to fill the air between us. Finally, Victoria said, "I think we should call him. Together."

Wrath looked dubious. "Call Cecil-Jace-Jeff? Just like that?"

A sly, unfriendly grin replaced Victoria's sneer. "No one knows more than I do about pretending to be someone you're not. Fake it till you make it, right? But even actors need something to go on. A little truth to sell the lie." She nodded as if confirming something to herself. "I'm the only person who can prove this Cecil character isn't who he says he is. I should have done it from the beginning, but I didn't want anyone to know who *I* really am. I like letting the debutantes of Odyssey think I'm one of them. But now you know my secret, so." She squared her shoulders and took a breath. "So are we doing this?"

Wrath turned the decision over to me with a lift of his shoulders and a glance. I sighed. "All right. Let's go someplace quiet."

Victoria beckoned for us to follow as she turned to head back toward town. "I have just the place."

———

The three of us plus Victoria's Labrador piled into her SUV and drove a few miles to our destination. We climbed out of the car and found ourselves in front of a café and bakery called Déjà Brew. Like many of Odyssey's shops, the exterior was pale turquoise with a pink-and-white striped awning and a glass door with a hand-painted image of a witch stirring a cauldron full of coffee.

Inside, a middle-aged man behind the counter dusted his hands on his apron. When he saw Victoria, he reached for a paper cup and headed toward the espresso machine. "Hey, Vic. What are you doing here? Today's not your day."

Victoria gestured toward the coffee cup in the man's hands and then drew her fingers across her throat in a cut-it-out motion. "No americano for me today, Felix. I'm not here for treats, unfortunately. I have some business to take care of." Felix placed the cup back on the stack and leaned against the counter as Victoria kept talking. "Do you mind hanging out with Charlie for a bit? You know how he gets when he goes downstairs."

Felix snapped his fingers and whistled. Charlie—the Labrador—trotted around the counter and lay obediently on the cool tile. As the dog got situated, Felix glanced at Wrath and me. "Who are your friends?"

Victoria straightened, sniffing importantly. "They're from that TV show filming in town. You know the one. Portia scoped out the property for the network." She turned to Wrath and me. "That was all Portia talked about for *weeks*, like finding a venue was the most important problem anyone could have. Really, it was *very* annoying." She redirected her attention to the barista. "*Sinful House?*"

The barista snapped his fingers, nodding with understanding. "Oh, that's right. I remember. Has it aired yet?"

I nodded. "Every weeknight at 8," I said.

"Anyway," Victoria interrupted, "I was hoping for some quiet time. I thought I'd take these two down to the Crypt. There's nobody else down there, is there?"

Felix shook her head. "Nope, empty. The whole basement's yours."

I blinked. "Basement?"

Wrath rolled his eyes. "Big, dark rooms underneath the house used for man-caves and storing garbage from the past most people should just get rid of," he explained.

"I know what a basement is," I sighed. "I've just never seen one in California."

Wrath shrugged. "Guess you're about to."

If you know much about Southern California, you already know it's not exactly the land of basements. (Contrary to popular belief, the lack of basements has nothing to do with earthquakes. It has more to do with the housing boom post World War II. It was just more expedient to build homes without them.) I had never seen a basement until I was in my late 20s and the police department sent me to Ohio on an investigation. So you can imagine my surprise when Victoria led us down a set of winding steps and through a wooden door that took us into the cool dark of my very first California basement.

And the surprises didn't stop there.

As my eyes adjusted to the chowdery darkness, shapes swam into view, coming together like puzzle pieces to form an incredible picture.

We were in some kind of underground lair.

That was the only word I could think to describe it.

The large, hexagonal room looked like something from a rich superhero's dungeon—if the superhero was really into esoterica, anyway. The walls were lined with bookshelves, but they hosted more than books. Crystal balls on silver pedestals sat nestled among live plants, candles of varying heights and colors, and mortars overflowing with herbs. An array of wands ranging from ornate pewter and amethyst to roughly hewn wooden sticks poked out from between book spines bearing titles such as *A Mage's Guide to Astronomy* and *Victorian Floriography for the Discerning Spiritualist*. The shelves were immaculate—not a speck of dust or even a wayward hair besmirched their appearance.

I looked up, marveling. The ceiling was painted to resemble the night sky, with shades from indigo to violet creating a backdrop for constellations illustrated with glittering metallic gold paint. In the center of the room were two long, dark wood tables covered in lamps and open books like you might find in an old Gothic library. In fact, the whole place very much gave off library vibes. Except for one thing.

The room was absolutely packed with ghosts.

Spirits faded in and out of translucence as they floated from one corner of the room to another. Some ghosts looked fully corporeal—I had to really examine them to see they were no longer living. Others were diaphanous shades of creamy blues and aquas. They seemed to come from different periods. Some looked freshly dead as they sported more modern looks. Others looked like they died some time ago—one ghost was wearing go-go boots and a beehive hairstyle. She had apparently died in a car accident. She was mangled, her body parts twisted in ways they weren't supposed to bend. Still, she was smiling ear to ear as she floated between clusters of spirits, moving from conversation to conversation with grace and ease.

I stood in mesmerized silence as my eyes followed them around the room. I'd never seen so many ghosts in one place. Finding a collection of spirits in the basement of a beachside cafe was enough to astound me. But their behavior, too, gave me pause. They were engaging with each other in ways I hadn't seen before. Sometimes, I came across pairs of ghosts—usually a husband and wife or sometimes siblings who had died together. But rarely did I see *groups* of ghosts. And never had I seen them mingling.

I mean, these ghosts were *cavorting*—traipsing about as if they were at their own private cocktail party.

It was curious. No, it was downright *weird*.

"What is this place?" Wrath asked as I continued to stare at the surrounding specters. An older woman in a long dress with a broken neck was laughing prettily with a pair of young men in fireproof racing suits. The two men were blackened, obviously burned to death.

I guess the suits were merely fire *retardant*.

"This is our headquarters," Victoria said. "We call it the Crypt because it's underground and because, well." She looked at me, head cocked to the side. "You tell me, Pride."

I looked at Wrath, eyebrows waggling. "This place is absolutely crawling with dead people."

Wrath froze, only his eyes darting around in the dark. "When you say dead people…You mean ghosts?"

I nodded. "Yeah. Dozens of them." I looked to Victoria. "This is some kind of ghost speakeasy."

Victoria's hand floated to the base of her throat as she laughed, a full sound that rattled my bones. "No one's ever called it that before, but I guess you're right. What an excellent description! Wait till I tell the others. Of course, *we* can't see them. But some of us are learning to sense them. Dozens, you say?" Victoria looked around with new interest, like this information might allow her to see what I saw. "They come from all around, I hear. Many of them are from Odyssey, of course, but I guess once word got around about our little haven, the other ghosts naturally found their way here. And we have no objections. I mean, really, a haunted sanctuary? You couldn't ask for a better setup."

Finding his voice again, Wrath cleared his throat and shook himself, no doubt shaking off a chill that shuddered through his body. "Exactly what kind of sanctuary is this? Headquarters for what?"

Victoria blinked in surprise. "The Society, of course. My apologies. I thought you knew. The Odyssey Para-normal Research Society. You met some of us gathered at the séance. We gather here regularly to compare notes and study. Among other things." She smiled, her eyes like sapphires in the shadows. "Anyway, this was the best place I could think of for some privacy to make a phone call." Victoria glanced between Wrath and me. "No objections?"

I pulled up Cecil's contact information on my phone

and handed it to Victoria. "Do you know what you're going to say? This is our only chance, you know. If you screw this up…"

Victoria grabbed the phone and made a dismissive sound in her throat. "I know what I'm doing," she said.

Victoria dialed with the phone on speaker. My breath caught in my throat as it rang. But it just went on ringing. Cecil never answered.

"Let's call Jace," Wrath suggested. "Calling him on his *real* phone number, which he never gave to Tamora, should let him know we mean business."

"We don't have Jace's phone number," I reminded him.

Wrath chuckled and pulled out his phone, holding it up to his mouth. "Do a deep web search for Jace Harris Thornburgh's phone number in San Francisco, California."

A second later, the browser displayed a profile, complete with phone number, Jace's picture, address, birth date, and the same information for his closest relatives.

And that's why you can't just put all your information out on the internet.

Wrath dialed and handed the phone to Victoria.

It rang for a long time, and I was sure it would go to voicemail. But then a voice answered.

"Hello?"

Victoria hesitated, licking her lips and swallowing. Then, she said, "Jeff? Oh my God, Jeff. Is it really you?"

Silence met us on the other line. Then, "Sorry, you have the wrong number."

Victoria tittered, turning her back to us. "No, wait, don't hang up." I couldn't see her face, but I heard the crack in her voice when she spoke. "It's me, Jeff. It's Victoria. We need to talk." She paused. *"They're back."*

The man on the other end sucked in a sharp breath. "Listen, lady, you have the wrong—"

"Oh, sorry. I might've mixed this all up in my silly head. Cecil, then? Is this Cecil?"

The man on the phone was silent, but he didn't hang up. Then he said, "Where did you get this number? Did Cecil give it to you?"

"No. I tried calling Cecil first, but he didn't answer. I wonder why that would be, Jace. Do you have any idea why he wouldn't answer his phone?"

Jace(?)/Cecil(?)/Jeff(?) sighed on the other end. "If you're trying to reach Cecil, he's…not here right now. But I can take a message."

Victoria snorted. "Oh, I just bet you can. I'm not actually looking for Cecil, though. I'm looking for Jeff Bishop. I understand Cecil knows where he is. I hear they've grown *close.*"

A long stretch of silence filled the air. Then he said, "Listen, Victoria? Is that what you said your name was? I think you have the wrong idea."

"Is this Jeff Bishop or not?" Victoria demanded.

The man on the other end sighed. "I—it's complicated. Can you please tell me who you are?"

Now, Victoria threw her shoulders back and lifted her chin, her eyes narrowed to slits. Her voice was smooth as ice when she said, "My name is Victoria Webster, and I'm close friends with Tamora Preston. I'm about to go to the police with everything I know about you. You're Jace Thornburgh, you're not Cecil Bradshaw, you're not a psychic medium, and you're trying to fleece my friend out of her fortune. You're a charlatan, and I can prove it. *You're not Jeff Bishop.*"

I froze, eyes darting to Wrath. He looked like I felt—cords in his neck stood out, his eyes wide and round. This was not what we had agreed to. Victoria was just supposed to pry into the poltergeists. But instead she was stealing our thunder.

The man sighed heavily. "No, I'm not. Not exactly."

"Are you the person my friend Tamora has been talking to or not? You owe me an explanation!"

"And I'm happy to give you one," the man said. He sounded weary. "But not over the phone. You wouldn't believe me if I did."

"You're probably right about that," Victoria spat. "So what do you propose? I don't think a video call will cut it."

"Cecil can come to Odyssey," the man said. "That's where you are, right?"

Victoria blinked in surprise. That was an answer none of us expected. "Really?"

"I knew—we both knew—it was only a matter of time before someone interfered in all this. I wasn't expecting anyone to call this number, but…Anyway, I need a few days to get my affairs in order. And I need to…scrape together the money for a plane ticket."

"Your expenses are on me," Victoria said importantly. "But this better not be another trick. I expect you here in Odyssey in a reasonable amount of time or I will call the police."

"I understand, and I appreciate the offer," the man said. "You have my number."

Then he hung up.

Victoria handed Wrath his phone and crossed her arms over her chest. "Well, that's done," she said. "Looks like we've caught ourselves a catfish."

"You were supposed to ask him about the poltergeists," Wrath grumbled. "But instead, you showed all our cards!"

"It doesn't matter," Victoria said with a shrug. "That guy is lying through his teeth, and if the two of you have any talent at all, you'll get him to confess everything on camera just like the network wants. You'll be heroes. Isn't that what you want?"

Wrath glowered but said nothing. I still didn't know what Wrath's ultimate desire was, so I had no idea why he'd come to Sinful House. He didn't strike me as hero-inclined.

But then, nobody at Sinful House was really who they seemed. If I'd learned anything on this show, it was that you can't take anyone at face value.

Victoria turned to leave, and with a sigh, Wrath followed her up the stairs, leaving me alone in a swirl of gossiping ghosts. I didn't want to admit it, but at that moment, the idea of being a hero lit something inside of me, and my heart skipped a beat.

Just don't tell anyone I said that.

# eleven

. . .

The next morning, Gluttony made breakfast tacos. He didn't put any magic in them, either, so I felt comfortable eating them. The "complimentary" muffins hadn't been the worst experience on earth, but you don't know how stupid it feels to walk around telling everybody how great they look and smell until it's actually happened to you. Seriously, try it if you don't believe me. People look at you like you've lost your mind.

Which says a lot about us as a society, I guess.

Anyway, I was waddling to my room after having stuffed my face with way too much sausage and eggs when I heard Sloth's voice call out my name.

I poked my head through her doorway and found her sitting cross-legged on her bed with Walt's computer in her lap. She was waving me over with a big smile on her face. "Pride, hey! You got a second? They reset the password for Walt's Chenoweth International account."

With everything else going on, I'd forgotten all about Mrs. Romanowsky and the case Sloth and I were supposed to be investigating on the side. I glanced down at my smartwatch. It was getting late, and I was tired, but for once, Sloth looked so upbeat that I couldn't turn away. So even though I wanted to lie down and wallow in my indigestion, I went into her room and plopped beside her on the bed.

"I just got the confirmation a few minutes ago," she explained. "I haven't even clicked on it yet."

I watched as she opened the email and clicked the shop link. The browser opened and the shopping page loaded up.

And, just as we expected, it was full of products for motorcycle enthusiasts. Helmets, jackets, other gear. Things like that. There were even parts for customizations.

In other words, completely worthless.

Sloth slumped beside me, the air going out of her like a deflated balloon. "This just doesn't make sense," she said. "I really thought we were going to find something more sinister."

"Sinister?" I asked. "Like how?"

Sloth laughed, her cheeks rosy. "I don't know, something like the Dark Web. You know what I mean?"

I drew my brows together, questioning. "You thought the motorcycle website was going to be a portal into the Dark Web?"

"What do you two dweebs know about the Dark Web?"

Sloth and I looked up to see Wrath coming into the room, a towel thrown over his shoulder. He was wearing board shorts with no shirt. Maybe he was going down to the beach later. Or it could be a fashion statement. You never could tell with Wrath. He ambled over to the bed and turned the laptop so he could see the screen. "What are you guys doing? Since when are you into motorcycles?" He shot me a dubious look when he caught me looking at his bare torso. "You're not going to tell me I have a beautiful chest, are you?"

"Shut up," I growled. "The spell wore off a long time ago."

"Well, thank goodness for that," he said, wiping a hand across his forehead in feigned relief. "Okay, but seriously, since when are you two into motorcycles?"

"We're *not* into motorcycles," Sloth said. "We're doing some sleuthing on the side." She quickly explained everything we knew so far about Walt Romanowsky, the organization, and Ping—the supe Walt had been hunting in Odyssey. She'd turned out to be a nine-tailed fox. "So we're trying to find out more about the organization Walt was involved with. We think he's hunting these creatures, but the email and website and everything are all about motorcycles. Here. Why don't you just look at the email yourself?"

Wrath pushed me aside, and Sloth and I made room for him on the bed. He took the computer into his lap and scrolled through the emails. He made quick work of them and then looked up at us, his eyes wide and round. "Are you two stupid or something?"

I jabbed Wrath in the side with my elbow and mouthed, *"Watch it!"* while jerking my head in Sloth's direction.

But Sloth rolled her eyes and dropped her chin into

her hand. "Don't worry, I've been called worse. So… why are you asking if we're stupid?"

Wrath gestured toward the computer screen. "This is the worst code I've ever seen."

Sloth and I exchanged looks. "Code? Like computer code? What are you talking about?"

Wrath buried his hands in his hair, shaking his head in disbelief. "I swear, the two of you are so gullible. Did you really read these emails and think they were literally talking about motorcycles? They're *obviously* talking about something else. The motorcycles are code. Geez, didn't you ever watch spy movies?"

Spy movies aside (I was much more of a science fiction fan myself), Wrath's words tickled something in the back of my brain. I clicked the shop link one more time, bringing up the motorcycle parts page. I thrust the computer back at Wrath. "Can you do some of that technopathy of yours and see if there's more to this website than meets the eye?"

Wrath clucked his tongue against his teeth. "With my eyes closed," he said. "Browser, show me all gated content."

A new browser window appeared. For a moment, the page flashed to the motorcycle homepage. Then a second page flashed with a pop-up window. The motorcycle parts and gear page displayed again.

Then, a new page rendered.

It was still a shopping page, but this time, there were no motorcycle parts or gear.

It was equipment for…animals.

Cages, collars, leashes, you name it—this page had it

all. As the three of us read over the descriptions, my heart tried to escape my chest. I pointed to a familiar product. "This is the cat carrier the cops found at the restaurant," I said. "Look at this description."

Wrath read it aloud. "Chenoweth Top Load Supe Carrier for Large and Medium Cats, Small Foxes, Small Tanuki, Small Dogs. Easy to get the supernatural in, and comfortable to carry, store, and clean. Chenoweth MagicBloc™ technology ensures supes can't escape or shift into another form while inside. The Top Load Supe Carrier comes with an adjustable shoulder strap for easy, hands-free carrying. It's also a cinch to store—just unzip and fold it down."

"You've got to be kidding me," Sloth breathed, her hand going to her mouth. "This whole motorcycle thing was a front. This is where Walter was getting his accessories. He was ordering them from this hidden website."

"Haha, check out this review," Wrath said, leaning forward as he continued to read. "3 stars. The Top Load Supe Carrier would be great except that, thanks to the MagicBloc™ technology, the carrier emits a slight glow when seen from the correct angle. If you're trying to fly under the radar, this isn't the carrier for you. Try the Front Load Supe Carrier with MagicThwart™ instead. It's not as convenient, but it doesn't glow."

I muttered something like, "Heh, that's funny," just to be polite, but I wasn't really listening. I was scanning the page, taking in as much information as possible. "What do you make of this?" I pointed to where the price should be for the cat carrier. "Says 5,000 points. Does that mean they don't accept cash?"

"You see that sometimes on these specialist commerce sites," Wrath said. "They use their own currency. It's points based. I'm guessing you earn points for completing certain tasks. When I worked in tech, our company gave us points for stuff like exercising regularly and completing our performance reviews on time. You could trade those points in for discounts on cell phone services, monitors, stuff like that. Or sometimes you could buy company swag with them."

I hrmmed, tapping my fingers thoughtfully against my chin. "Interesting. So, like, the more supernaturals you catch, the more points you get?"

"Or the rarer the catch," Wrath supplied. "Quality over quantity."

"I wonder what the motorcycles are code for," Sloth mused. "Maybe they're unicorns or—"

"Unicorns?" I snorted. "Come on."

"I don't see why *that's* so far-fetched," she said. "Not after everything else."

She had a point, but I wasn't willing to concede it. My worldview was still too small to include unicorns. "I wonder if the type of motorcycle is significant. He said they were SuperHawks. You think that matters?"

Wrath shrugged. "Don't know, but whatever the motorcycles really are, sounds like Walt never unloaded them. At least, not to this guy. Do you know where his 'garage' is?"

Sloth shook her head. "No. But maybe his mom knows?"

"We should definitely ask her," I agreed. "Let's make time to go chat with her, okay?" While Sloth scribbled something down on a wayward receipt she was apparently using for a to-do list, I leaned over to Wrath. "Hey, is this the only gated page you found?"

My housemate shook his head. "No, look. There's a bunch. They're just in different tabs." He clicked over to the next tab and barked out a sharp laugh. "Well, there you go."

The page was titled, "Chenoweth Point Awards". It was broken down into a grid. In each cell was a photo of a creature, a name, a description, and the number of points each creature was worth.

"Look at this," I said, scrolling to the middle of the page. "The nine-tailed fox is worth 25,000 points."

"That's less than I would have thought," Sloth said. "That equals only five cat carriers."

"That's how they screw you," Wrath sneered. "They're stingy with the points they give out, and overcharge for the products you buy. That's why private currency is a slippery slope toward exploitation, man. It's not fair when the company owns both the product *and* the currency."

"Well, I'm not going to lose any sleep over people hunting supernatural creatures getting shafted," I admitted. "Is there any contact information anywhere on the site? An address, a phone number? Something like that?"

Wrath touched the screen. "Browser, show me physical addresses, phone numbers, and email addresses associated with this URL."

The browser returned nothing but the "Request Account/Reset Password" page we'd already visited.

"Doesn't look like it," Wrath said. "Whoever these people are, they're not interested in random jerks reaching out to them. But." He grinned, a mischievous look in his eye. "I bet if you make enough noise, they'll find you."

"Make noise how?" Sloth asked.

"I don't know, and I'm too busy to think about it right now," he said. "I've got a lot to do today." He stood, stretched, and walked to the door.

I looked up. "You do?"

"I've got, like, two raids to do with my guild, and I have to earn back the honor points I lost when you kicked me out of that PvP match."

"Gaming," I said. "You're busy with *gaming*."

"You got a problem with that?"

I shrugged. "It's your life. Waste it how you want."

Wrath paused in the doorway. "Leisure time is not time wasted. There you go again, Pride, equating value with production. Life is meant to be enjoyed, man. You can't gauge the value of your life based on capitalist—"

I shoved Wrath into the hallway and closed the door.

With Wrath gone, Sloth returned her attention to me. "I want to go talk to Mrs. Romanowsky today. Do you want to come with me?"

I gave a noncommittal shrug. "I've got time. When were you thinking of heading over?"

Her face brightened. "Right now!"

I glanced down at her outfit. She was wearing a t-shirt three sizes too big that looked like she'd slept in it. Her shorts used to be sweatpants, but she'd cut them off at the knee. They were covered in various stains and tattering along the edge. "Is that what you're wearing?" I asked.

Sloth's mouth twisted into a tight moue and her brows drew together sharply. "Not you, too," she scolded. "Do I exist just as an object of beauty for other people to admire? I don't think so," she said. "I'm allowed to look slovenly and sloppy if I want to. I don't owe you my attractiveness. Besides—beauty is only skin deep."

I blushed, chagrined. I'd heard Wrath giving Sloth this lecture a few days ago. She'd been crying in the bathroom—a sight I was getting used to, unfortunately—and when Wrath asked her what was wrong, she said some local women were making fun of her appearance. Wrath had gone into a full-blown tantrum, ranting that people rarely made such comments to men but felt free to hurl them at women. "Don't take that garbage from anyone, man," he admonished, his index finger pointing in Sloth's face. "Antagonizing women for their looks is patriarchal nonsense, Sloth. Self-confidence is punk rock, man. Loving yourself is a rebellion. Dress how you like. Do what you want. It's your life, after all."

"You're right," I said. "You don't owe anyone anything. And good for you for sticking up for yourself."

Her smile grew so bright, I could have used her face as a flashlight.

Almost skipping with joy, Sloth led the way out the front door, and a few minutes later, we were on our way to visit Eleanor Romanowsky.

# twelve

. . .

When we arrived at the Romanowsky place, Sloth rang the doorbell.

As we waited on the porch, I studied the street. The last time I was here, I'd run into a pair of ghosts, the spirits of a couple who had drowned. I didn't see them today, which meant nothing, of course. Ghosts didn't usually hang out in the same place unless they were haunting it. But that got me thinking about the headquarters for the Society. Why were those ghosts hanging out there? How did they find out about the place? Were they haunting it? It sure didn't seem like a standard haunting to me. Not that I'm an expert, but still.

Just as I was slipping deeper into these thoughts, Sloth grunted at my side. "Why isn't she answering?" She jabbed the doorbell several times with her thumb. But again, nothing happened.

With the laptop tucked against her side, Sloth began knocking on the door. "Mrs. Romanowsky?" she called out. "Are you in there?"

"Did you tell her we were coming?" I asked. "It doesn't look like she's home."

Sloth stood up straight and blew out a noisy breath through her nose. "She hardly leaves the house," she said. "That's why she gets so lonely, remember? But I guess it's possible. Let's go check the garage."

We walked around the side of the house to the attached garage. The windows were caked in dust and about a thousand years' worth of dirt. I shielded my eyes to peer inside. I could barely make out Eleanor Romanowsky's Cadillac—or, at least, someone's Cadillac. It could have been Walt's for all we knew. But it was a Cadillac, after all, which mostly only old people drive.

Listen, when you're investigating mysteries, sometimes stereotypes are helpful.

"Her car's here," I said. "But maybe someone picked her up. Does she use rideshares?"

Sloth gave me a look. "How should I know?" She shifted her weight, chewing on her lips thoughtfully. "No, Pride, something's not right."

We marched back around to the front of the house. Once more, Sloth banged on the door, calling out for Mrs. Romanowsky. When no one answered, I tried the doorknob.

The door swung open.

I started to enter, but Sloth put her free hand on my shoulder, tugging me back. "Hang on. Doesn't seem right to just barge in." She leaned her head through the door. "Mrs. Romanowsky? Are you—"

She didn't have time to complete the question,

however. With the door open, we had an unobstructed view of the main hall leading into the living room.

The interior was destroyed. It looked like a giant had picked up the house and shaken it like a snow globe. Paintings that used to hang on the wall lay in a shattered heap on the floor. Furniture was overturned. I reached for my housemate. "Sloth—"

But before I could grab her, Sloth darted into the house. I followed on her heels, taking in the wreckage. The further we drew into the house, the colder my blood ran. Something terrible had happened here. And I had a feeling things were only going to get worse.

When we entered the living room, Sloth screamed.

I was right.

Mrs. Romanowsky lay in the middle of the living room floor, her body a crumpled heap. Like the hallway, the living room was ruined. Books, knickknacks, and dishes lay scattered over the floor amid trashed furniture. Someone had taken a blade to the upholstery and ripped out the insides. Cotton stuffing and shredded foam were everywhere. As I stood there surveying the damage, Sloth dropped to her knees at Eleanor's side. She pressed her fingers against the woman's throat, looking for a pulse. But when she looked up at me, her eyes were filled with tears.

"She's dead," Sloth said.

I nodded, pointing to the wound on her chest. "Yeah. She's been shot."

As if suddenly realizing we were in the middle of a crime scene, Sloth jumped to her feet, covering her mouth with her hand. "Oh, Pride. What if they're still in the house? What if they're still here and they know we're here and—"

Her voice was rising in a panic, so I grabbed her by the shoulders and shook her, forcing her to focus on me. "Nobody's here," I said. "We're alone, okay? We're alone."

"How do you know?" she said, her eyes still wild with fright. "How do you—"

"Because Eleanor's been dead a while. At least a day. Look at the corpse, Sloth. You can tell by the way —what?"

Sloth looked like she might throw up, the color draining from her face. "Don't explain," she said. "I shouldn't have asked. There's no…there aren't any other minds around, or I'd be able to hear their thoughts. It's just us."

I didn't think she would start screaming again, so I released her. She didn't move. "What do we do?" she asked. "Do we call the cops?"

I looked around and nodded. "Yes, obviously. We call the cops. I don't know what happened here, but it looks like someone was looking for something. This looks like a robbery, and poor Eleanor was just collateral damage."

Sloth swallowed and began to tremble, her teeth clattering. She was going into shock. "Collateral damage," she echoed, bemused. "She was a *person*, Pride. Not collateral damage. She was murdered in her own home just weeks after her son was killed."

A voice drifted into the room. "I'm pretty sure the two are related."

I looked up to find the ghost of Eleanor Romanowsky hovering at the far edge of the room. Her face was despondent, her eyes trained on her own corpse. "It's the only thing that makes sense," she said.

Gingerly, I stepped away from Sloth and toward the ghost, neatly avoiding the body in the middle of the floor. "I doubt that," I said flatly. "Walt's death was mostly an accident. You were…" I gestured vaguely toward the body. "You were obviously murdered."

Behind me, I heard movement, and a moment later, Sloth was pressed against my side. "Pride? Who are you talking to?"

I gestured at the ghost, but all Sloth could see was empty air. Her eyes searched the space but latched on to nothing. "It's Eleanor," I said. "Her ghost is here."

Sloth's eyes went wide as she pressed her hand to her mouth. "Mrs. Romanowsky? She's here?"

I nodded. "That's what I said."

Sloth stepped toward the ghost, and Eleanor backed away. For some reason, that struck me as funny. Even in death, people don't like having others inside their bubble. "Can you tell her something for me? Can you tell her I'm still trying to help?"

I smiled. "She can hear you," I said. "You can't hear her. But she can hear you."

Eleanor reached a hand toward Sloth in response, but her spectral form passed through Sloth's body. Eleanor paused, lifting her hand to her face, then tried again. Still her hand passed through Sloth. She shuddered, depressed, and let her hand fall limply to her side.

"Please tell her I appreciate everything she has done for me so far."

I relayed the message to Sloth before returning my attention to Eleanor. "Did you see what happened here? Who did this? And why do you think it's related to Walt's death?"

In response, Eleanor lifted a hand and pointed toward the second floor. "They took my birds," she answered, her voice wavering.

I blinked in surprise. "Your birds? I don't get it. Why—"

But then I understood.

Suddenly, everything came crashing into my skull at once. The last time I'd been at this house, I'd noticed the birdcage glowing. Not all the time, and not if I looked directly at it. But if I looked at it from the corner of my eye, it glowed.

And then I remembered the cat carrier listing on the Chenoweth website. One commenter had mentioned that the MagicBloc™ technology had a visible glow.

"Your birds were shapeshifters," I said. "That cage was magic. It kept them from shifting. Did you know?"

Eleanor's hands were at her throat, her fingers winding around the delicate gold chain at her neck. "I didn't, not until the men came. But they were wearing outfits just like Walter used to wear. And I put two and two together. My son was a supernatural bounty hunter —and all this time, I had supernaturals in my house, and I didn't even know it." Again, she gestured toward her upstairs bedroom. "One of them went straight upstairs when they heard the birds twittering. I tried to stop him. That's when…" She looked down at her ruined chest. "That's when he shot me."

I looked at Sloth. "The SuperHawks," I breathed. "The birds were the SuperHawks."

Eleanor was speaking again, but I wasn't listening. I had to see for myself. I darted up the stairs and into Eleanor's bedroom. At the foot of her luxurious canopy bed was a giant birdcage. Someone had taken a pair of wire cutters and cut a hole into the cage. The two red and gold sun conures that had once chirped noisily from the cage were gone.

Back downstairs, Eleanor was floating around the living room, still wringing her hands in worry. When she saw me, she stilled. "You see? They're gone."

"Eleanor, I need you to think. What can you tell me about what happened here? Let's start with—how many people were here?"

Eleanor nodded. "Two. Two men, and they were looking for something. As I lay on the floor bleeding to death, they kept shouting at me, asking me where it was. But of course, I couldn't answer. And I had no incentive to, anyway. I knew I was dying."

I held out my hands, pleading. "What were they asking about, Eleanor? What were they looking for?"

Eleanor chewed her lips, glancing nervously between Sloth and me before she said, in a voice almost too quiet for me to hear, "Walter's laptop."

Stark dread washed over me, and I grabbed Sloth by the wrist. "We have to get out of here," I said.

Sloth stared, too scared to move. "Why? What did she say? Pride, tell me what's going on!"

"I'll explain later," I said. "We're in danger here."

I was heading for the door when Eleanor's voice stopped me in my tracks. "I know I'm dead," she called. "But please don't leave me here. I've been too afraid to leave on my own, and I don't know why I haven't gone to the other side. But I don't want to stay in this house with my own dead body a moment longer. Please. Please take me with you."

I paused only long enough to instruct Sloth to get into the car immediately. While Sloth hurried out of the house, I stalked over to Eleanor and gazed into her eyes. They were liquid and rheumy, but even in death, I saw the despair in them. "I don't know how to do this," I said. "I can't touch ghosts. And you can't touch me."

As if testing that theory, the old woman reached out to me. As had happened so many times before, I expected her hand to pass right through my body.

But it didn't.

Her fingers latched onto my wrist. An icy chill ran down my spine. The pressure on my skin where her fingertips met my flesh was unnerving. This wasn't right. I'd known my fair share of ghosts, and none of them, not one, could touch me.

But Eleanor was grasping me. I felt her trembling.

"Come on, then," I said, tugging the ghost toward the door. Unbelievably, she followed.

I darted from the house, dragging a petrified ghost behind me. As soon as we were inside the car, I started the engine while Sloth dialed the police. Then I stepped on the gas, and we flew out of there.

# thirteen

. . .

"Where are we going, Pride? This isn't the way home."

I eased up a bit on the gas, my heart no longer throbbing in my ears. The more distance we got from Eleanor's house, the more confident I felt no one had seen us go in. No one knew we had the laptop.

I threw a sidelong glance at Sloth and sucked in a sharp breath. "We need to take Eleanor somewhere safe," I said. "I don't think Sinful House is the right place for her. She needs to be around others of her kind."

Sloth's eyes grew wide as she looked around the car. It's so funny when people do that. You tell them a ghost is around and they look for it, even though they know they can't see it. Human nature is wild sometimes.

"Take her—She's here? In the car?"

I jerked my head towards the backseat. "Sitting right next to the cameraman," I said.

The camera guy let out a little squeal as he squished

himself into the corner, giving the ghost as wide a berth as possible. I chuckled under my breath.

"Why did you bring her? Not that I mind," Sloth said quickly, "it just seems like maybe she'd be better off at her house."

I shook my head. "Number one, she said she didn't want to stay there. But number two, if the people we're looking for—the same people who killed Eleanor—are supernatural bounty hunters, I figure they may have some knowledge about ghosts, too. The last thing I want is for them to get their hands on Eleanor. I don't know if you can torture a ghost. But I also don't want to find out."

I wasn't sure if my words made everyone feel better or worse, but it was the truth. I glanced at Eleanor in the rear-view mirror. "I won't let anything happen to you," I promised.

The ghost nodded mutely.

I parked outside Déjà Brew, and as the camera guy opened his door, I shook my head. "You're staying here," I said. "I can't let you in there."

The camera man gestured wildly toward the empty air in the backseat. "I'm not sitting in here alone with a ghost. The network doesn't pay me enough—"

"Calm down, compadre. The ghost is coming with me and Sloth. You're staying here alone."

Relief flooded his face, but he still gave me a petulant frown for show. "Network won't like it," he said.

I slammed the door, and Eleanor latched onto my wrist as I tugged her forward. "They'll live."

Inside the café, Felix was wiping down the counter,

and the smell of espresso filled the air. Unlike the previous time I'd been at Déjà Brew, the place was filled with patrons. When he saw us, Felix straightened and dropped the rag to the counter. I'd like to say he was glad to see me, but that would be a lie. He looked perplexed.

"Hey, Felix," I said. "I hate to bother you. Do you remember me from the other day?"

The barista's eyes darted between Sloth and me as he fidgeted. "I remember you," he said cautiously. "You were here with Victoria."

I nodded. "Listen, can we talk in private? I need a favor."

Felix smirked and ran a hand through his hair. "I'm not usually keen on granting favors to people I barely know. However…" He glanced at our group again. "Why don't you come with me into the back." He pointed to Sloth. "The rest of you stay here."

I followed Felix into the back, and he closed the door that separated the kitchen area from the main house. Now that we were alone, he folded his arms across and pitched his voice low. "What happened to Mrs. Romanowsky?" he asked. "Why is she *dead?*"

My mouth fell open. "I – how did you—wait. Can you see ghosts?"

Again, Felix smirked. "You didn't think I'd operate a haunted guild hall from my basement without the ability to monitor what's going on, did you? Of course I can see them. Until you arrived, I was the only person in Odyssey who could. So, while I don't exactly think of you as a rival, I'm wary about you. To say the least."

Well, that tracked. I was wary of most people in Odyssey, too. "I see. Well, I need your help. Some dangerous people broke into Eleanor's house looking for something. When she didn't cooperate, they shot her. I don't know exactly what's going on," I admitted, "but I know Eleanor is better off here. I just get the feeling this place is safe. And I *know* her house isn't."

Felix dipped his chin toward his chest as he thought over what I'd said. He had no reason to trust me. After all, I was carting around the ghost of a murdered woman, the mother of a supernatural bounty hunter. But I'd come in with Victoria, and Victoria and Felix were friends. I think. It was hard to tell. People in this town weren't always what they appeared.

Navigating the waters of Odyssey isn't for the faint of heart. I don't recommend it to anyone.

"Here's what we're gonna do," Felix said. His voice sounded like he'd rolled it in gravel. "Take her down to the basement, but don't tell anyone she's here. We don't need to attract any attention. Did anybody see you come here? Do you think anybody followed you from the house?"

I shrugged, digging my hands into my pockets. "I don't know. I don't think so. By the time we found Eleanor, she'd been dead for at least a day. I don't think the bad guys hung around that long. But I've been wrong before," I admitted.

Felix stroked his chin, still thoughtful. Finally, he said, "I guess that's a chance we'll just have to take. Take her downstairs. Like I said. Mum's the word."

I followed Felix back into the café, where he donned

a cheerful grin for his patrons. I gestured for Sloth and Eleanor to follow me through the same doorway Victoria led me through. Quietly, we descended into darkness.

When we emerged into the Crypt, Sloth had the same reaction I did. Her eyes were wide as saucers as she wandered reverently through the room, taking in all the various accouterments of magic. She seemed especially enchanted by the astrology-painted ceiling.

But even more enthralled with this discovery was Eleanor. As soon as we were downstairs, she gasped audibly, freezing in her tracks as she took it all in. She was less interested in the wands and glass globes, though.

She was mesmerized by the ghosts.

"What is this place?" she whispered. "Are they all… like me? Are they all…?"

"They're all dead," I confirmed, nodding. "I don't know what they're doing here. But I thought if you can't stay home, you may as well have company."

Eventually, the other ghosts noticed they had a new member. Some kept their distance, surveying her from afar. But others were upon her like moths to flame, peppering her with questions.

"Eleanor? Is that you? Oh, come here, honey. Let me look at you!"

"Shot?! Who shot you? We need gun control in this country."

"Oh, my goodness, is everything okay? Of course it's not okay. You're dead."

"Mrs. Romanowsky, I'm so sorry to see you here. I

thought you'd never die. I always said you would outlive us all! Which, I guess you did. Technically."

While Sloth examined her surroundings and Eleanor mingled with her new roommates, I scanned the room for ghosts who were more standoffish. A younger woman approximately my age stood watchful in the corner, her expression guarded. When I approached her, she stepped back, pressing herself against the wall. I stopped and held up my hands. "I don't want to hurt you," I said. Not that I could if I *did* want to. "My name's Pride. I thought I could ask you some questions."

The woman scoffed and raised an eyebrow. "Your name's Pride? What's the matter? Your mom not like you or something?"

I balked. "I never met my mother. She disappeared when I was an infant. But not because she didn't like me. At least, I have no proof of that."

The ghost looked like she was biting back a laugh. Then she said, "I'm Angelica Muñoz."

"Nice to meet you, Angelica." I didn't offer my hand, for obvious reasons. But no matter how many times I introduce myself to ghosts, it never stops feeling strange. "Can I ask you about this place? For starters, how long have you been down here?"

Angelica looked thoughtful, her image shimmering before my eyes. She must have been pretty in life. Her complexion was clear, her hair long and dark.

"It's hard to say," she breathed. "Once you're dead, time renders differently. I choked to death at a dinner party," she explained. "I kept waiting for that bright light everyone says you see when you die. But I never saw that. All I saw was my dead body lying on the ground while everyone around me cried and whatnot. Can you even imagine how disconcerting that is?" She huffed, turning up her nose. "Of course you can't. Why am I even asking? Anyway, I followed the ambulance toward the hospital before I realized—I'm dead. So I should make the most of it. You know. See the world."

She laughed then—at least I think it was a laugh. Her expression was very hard to read. "Turns out, though, traveling as a ghost is difficult, scary, and slow. At least for me. But as I was wandering the streets of Odyssey, I felt something call out to me."

I shivered, transfixed. "What was it?"

"It's hard to explain. It was like a voice in my head telling me where to go. So I walked—do ghosts walk? I guess I floated—until I found the place. It was a coffee shop, of all things, and I didn't even drink coffee in life. But Felix was there. He could see me. He welcomed me to the café and instructed me to go downstairs to where the others were. So here I am. I'm happy here, so I've never left. Although, I do much prefer it when the Society isn't in session. It gets so crowded. And it's already crowded enough. Even more so now that you've brought us another one."

"She had nowhere else to go," I pointed out.

Angelica sighed. "None of us do," she agreed.

I suddenly felt overwhelmed. Now that my adrenaline was wearing off, I felt my situation acutely. Mrs. Romanowsky had been murdered over a laptop now in Sloth's possession. My stomach felt sick, and my head was buzzing. I needed to go home and think. I thanked

Angelica and went to find Sloth. She was hunched over a book titled *Fairies, Cats, and Other Annoying Creatures*. I tapped her on the shoulder. "Sloth. We need to go."

She glanced up from the book and blinked. She looked like she'd forgotten where she was. "Is everything okay?"

"Yes, but I need to get out of here and lie down for a while."

Sloth closed the book and slid it back into place on the bookshelf. She turned around and shouted in the shadows. "I'll come visit you, Eleanor," Sloth promised. "You're in good hands here."

Eleanor nodded, waving goodbye. "Thank you for all your help, dears. Please be safe."

We said nothing more as we went upstairs. Sloth thanked Felix, and then we headed home to Sinful House.

———

That night, I went to bed early, but I couldn't sleep. Sometime after midnight, I rolled over onto my back, my arm draped across my forehead. I was staring at the ceiling and contemplating going downstairs for a glass of warm milk when the air cooled, and a familiar shape shimmered into view.

"You did good today, you know."

The ghost was sitting cross-legged on top of my comforter, her chin propped atop her knuckles. I grinned in the darkness. "I did, didn't I?"

She nodded. "Eleanor would've been stuck in that

house for a long time if you hadn't rescued her. You did the right thing taking her to Déjà Brew. She'll be happy there."

I rolled over onto my side, my cheek propped against my fist. I peered at the ghost, giving her a quizzical look. "How did you know about that? I mean, seriously, do you just follow me around in invisible mode all day? How do you know so much about my activities?"

The ghost giggled, covering her mouth with her free hand. "I'm psychic, silly."

"Psychic. Right." I knew that was a lie, but if she didn't want to let me in on her secrets, I wouldn't press the issue. "So I guess you saw me dragging her to the car. What I don't understand is how I could do that at all. You've tried to touch me a thousand times, but your hand always passes right through me."

The ghost reached out to pat me on the head, but as usual, her hand passed right through. "That is weird," she agreed. "I wonder how she was able to grab you."

"She tried to touch Sloth, but she couldn't," I said. "Is that normal?"

The ghost shrugged her slim little shoulders. "I don't know. I'm not an expert on ghosts."

"But you're a ghost," I chided. "So…?"

"You're a human," she retorted. "Are you an expert on humans?"

I chuckled. I guess she had a point there.

"Anyway," she said, switching her chin to her other hand, "Whatcha gonna do next? How are you gonna find those birds?"

I flopped onto my back and squeezed my eyes shut.

"I'm not going to look for the birds," I said. I heard a sharp intake of breath, but I remained still. "It's too dangerous. Believe me, I've done nothing but think about this all day. But they killed Eleanor. Shot her in cold blood over a laptop. Listen, I have no idea what's on the computer, but I can tell you one thing. I'm not willing to die over it."

The ghost inched closer to me, and I could feel her disapproval radiating off her tiny spectral body. "You can't just quit," she said. "Eleanor was counting on you. Are you just going to tell her that her death wasn't important enough for you to look into?"

I grunted, sucking my teeth in annoyance. "Of course not. The cops will handle it. I know they're not the most talented police force in America, but they'll look into it. They'll do more than I can do, anyway."

The ghost threw up her hands in exasperation. "You don't know that! You know about the missing parrots and the laptop. The cops don't. They can't talk to ghosts like you can. They can't interview Eleanor. They'll probably treat it just like a typical robbery, and justice will never get served. And more importantly, nobody will ever find those poor birds."

I swallowed hard, squeezing my eyes even tighter. "I've thought about all of that," I repeated. "But it's just getting to be too much. It's too dangerous."

"Did you know sun conures can mimic human speech? They can also mimic telephones ringing and car horns, too."

"I didn't know that," I answered, relieved we were changing the subject. If she wanted to talk all night about babbling birds, I'd let her. If it meant we were done talking about the Chenoweth investigation, I'd stay up until the sun.

"You're scared. That's your problem."

So much for that.

I laughed, a bitter, dry sound that felt out of place. "Of course I'm scared! Someone was murdered! I'm way outside my league here."

"You handled cases like this all the time when you worked with the San Diego police force. So what's different now?"

I turned my head to face her. "The difference is, I was just a consultant. I didn't chase bad guys. Detective Hidalgo did that. And he had a gun."

The ghost shrugged as if this were the sorriest excuse she'd ever heard. "So get a gun."

I returned my gaze to the ceiling. "It's not that simple."

"You're scared, so you're giving up. I thought you were better than that."

I slapped my hands against the mattress. "And what would you have me do, O Bodiless One With No Skin In The Game? I have nothing to go on. I don't know who those men were, I don't know where to find Chenoweth, and even if I did—I'm not cut out for this. I'm just not."

"I don't believe you."

"Feel free to leave," I said, gesturing toward the door. "I'm trying to sleep, anyway."

But instead of leaving, the ghost inched closer. "What are you going to tell Sloth?"

"We already discussed it. And she agrees it's too dangerous. She's going to hand the laptop over to the police, and then we'll both be done with this. It's better and safer for everyone this way." I hissed out a long sigh. I didn't know why I bothered to justify myself to a ghost who wasn't even old enough to drive.

Silence filled the air between us. I rolled onto my other side, away from the ghost. After a while, I probed the air with my ghost whisperer senses, and I found nothing.

I was once again alone.

With a huff, I punched my pillow. I didn't owe Eleanor my safety. I didn't.

So why did I feel so guilty?

"I made the smart decision," I said into the night, hoping hearing my words aloud would convince me they were true. "Just because a ghost thinks I'm a coward doesn't mean I am."

Only silence answered me. I tugged the blanket up under my chin and squeezed my eyes shut. But the ghost's words echoed in my ears for a long time. It wasn't until pale sunlight struggled through my bedroom curtains in the early morning that I found sleep too much to resist and finally faded away.

# fourteen

. . .

My phone rang early the next morning. Groggily, I answered, my eyes barely open. "Hello?"

"Good news," a woman's voice chirped. I didn't recognize it. "Cecil Bradshaw—or whoever he really is—will be in Odyssey in two days."

I rolled onto my back and shut my eyes. "Good morning, Victoria. That's great news. He has a ticket and everything?"

"Yes, everything's confirmed. I just got off the phone with him. Here's the kicker, though. He called from Cecil's phone number, but the man I spoke to was definitely *not* Jace Thornburgh."

I frowned. "What do you mean?"

"His voice was different. Similar, but different. It wasn't the same man we spoke to in the Crypt. At this point, I have no idea what that means. So what's the plan?"

I opened my eyes, brow wrinkled. "Plan?"

She sighed. "Yes, Pride. You need a *plan*. A little

*showmanship*. How do you plan to confront him and get everything on camera in the most TV-pleasing way possible?"

I yawned and stretched. It was too early for this. "I don't know, Victoria. I hadn't really thought about it."

"Well, I have," she said. "You need to host a dinner party."

I sighed. There are three things I hate more than anything:

1. Shopping
2. Being woken up at the crack of dawn by people I barely know trying to get me to do things I don't want to do, and
3. Dinner parties.

"I don't know if that's such a great idea," I mused.

"Why not?" She sounded indignant.

"Because I don't want to," I admitted.

Victoria's response was something between a laugh and a sigh. "I'll make this very easy on you. I've already thought it out. Just listen."

While Victoria rattled off the details of her cockamamie dinner party plan, I hauled myself out of bed and got dressed. I definitely needed a shower and to brush my teeth, but I'd slept badly, and I wanted coffee more than anything. So while Victoria talked, I walked downstairs.

I found Envy in the kitchen. She had a shopping bag slung over her shoulder. "Morning," she said, her voice all sing-song and awake and slightly annoying. "How'd you sleep?"

I gestured to the phone and mouthed, "Busy."

But Envy kept talking. "I'm making a run to the grocery store," she said. "I could use your company. There's something I want to talk to you about."

Since the phone gesture didn't work, I held up a finger to quiet her. Into the phone, I said, "Yeah, that's fine, Victoria. No, I appreciate it. Seriously. It's just early and you caught me sleeping. Yeah, sure, I'll tell him. No, thanks a lot. Yeah, I'll see you."

I clicked the phone to disconnect and jammed it in my pocket. "What were you saying?"

Envy shoved a bag into my hand. "Grocery store. I'd like to get some alone time with America's Favorite Sin."

I groaned. "I wish you'd stop saying that."

Envy poked out her tongue. "The fact that it bugs you is exactly why I still say it. Didn't you go to grammar school?

I ignored her the entire way to the grocery store.

Inside, I volunteered to push the cart. Envy tapped a finger against her lips, eyes scanning the items on her list. "We can probably cut this in half if we let one of my elementals help."

I spun around on my heel and pointed a finger in Envy's face. "Absolutely not," I said. "First of all, do you think the citizens of Odyssey are ready for one of your elementals? It's one thing to have them around the house. It's another thing for them to be tearing around town on their own."

My housemate made an exasperated sound as she

rolled her eyes. "Ugh, you're so dramatic. Don't worry. I'm not using the water or air elementals—they couldn't help, anyway. They're worthless at shopping. We'll use my earth elemental. And before you object," she said, holding up a hand, "he's not conspicuous. Unless you look *really* closely, he just looks like a short man. A very short man with round hips and a pointed hat," she amended under her breath, eyes darting sideways at me as she blushed. "But the earth elemental isn't even worthy of a second glance," she said in her usual speaking voice. "Usually."

"Number two," I said, continuing my objection, "the last time you summoned elementals to our house, the fire department ended up on our street. Don't you think you've caused enough trouble with them?"

Envy huffed, popping a hand on her hip as she narrowed her eyes at me. "If I don't keep summoning them, how am I supposed to get better at it? Besides. Back home, I *never* had any problems with the elementals. It's only since I've been in Odyssey that things have gone cockeyed. I'm not exactly sure why that is," she admitted, "but it's nothing a little practice can't fix. Trust me, Pride." She pressed her hand to her chest as she said this, offering me her best innocent smile. "It'll be fine."

When Envy had her mind made up, there was little I could say to dissuade her. So I dropped the subject and started pushing the cart. "What's the first item on the list?" I asked.

"Chicken," she said, her nose wrinkling, eyes scanning the rest of the list. "Why did I put chicken first?"

I shot her a confused glance. "Should chicken not be first?"

"Not on this list," she explained. "An unordered list just makes shopping tedious. Some people like to organize alphabetically, but even that's kind of a waste. I usually organize my list by shopping aisle. It's so much more efficient that way."

We were walking past an end cap filled with snack cakes. Envy grabbed one and threw it in the basket.

I shot her a look. "I thought the point of having a shopping list was so you didn't make impulse purchases," I chided.

Envy glanced sidelong at me, her lips pursed in displeasure. "I make lists so I don't forget things I need. That doesn't prevent me from buying things I *want*. Not that it matters. Every time I buy snack cakes, they disappear before I have a chance to eat them."

I recalled Gluttony eating my Chinese food out of the fridge without even an ounce of shame. "If you want something to yourself, you have to hide it. Gluttony has no boundaries."

Envy hrmmed as she selected a second package. "I'll keep that in mind. Anyway, listen. There's something I wanted to talk to you about."

We were headed towards the butcher for the chicken, which was on the other side of the grocery store. We walked past several displays—each containing nothing on our list—and Envy absently selected items from the shelves, tossing them into the basket. After throwing her third box of Velveeta into the cart, I stopped and looked her in the eye. "Envy. What's on your mind?"

Envy curled her lip beneath her teeth and sucked in a breath before answering. "Lust showed me that tiara you bought for her," she began slowly. "It's really nice. You chose well. I mean, I think wearing a tiara at our age is kind of weird, but that's not the point. She wanted it, and you bought it. Which was really nice. But which also raises some questions."

At the mention of my exchange with Lust, my stomach clenched. My personal business was my personal business, and I didn't really want to discuss it with Envy. This was stupid for several reasons, mainly because my personal business was being aired on TV, anyway. In fact, all over America, bloggers, vloggers, and influencers of all stripes were commenting on my personal life with wild abandon. As part of our contract, the network sent us updates on how we were being perceived in media—the "media" being everyone with a social media account. It's crazy to read strangers' opinions about yourself. They speculate and jump to wild conclusions. For example, there was an entire subReddit dedicated to analyzing our show, and several Redditors had posited that Shayda and I were never really together. That our entire relationship was a sham invented by the network to make me more sympathetic and normal.

It wasn't a bad theory. When it came to sympathy, I needed all the help I could get.

But that didn't make the theories true.

"So, what's your question?" I asked cautiously.

"You came on the show because you wanted to get

your girlfriend back, yeah? But you and Lust seem to be developing something. Which is fine," she hurried to add. "But Lust is my friend. So I just wonder if your intentions about her are pure."

We were passing by aisle 7, which contained bread and bread-related items. Envy had dinner rolls on her list, so I started to turn down the aisle. But Envy grabbed me by the elbow. "We're shopping the list in order," she said. "That's exactly why it should be organized when you…"

Her voice trailed off as she stared. Halfway down aisle 7, a short man wearing blue knickerbockers, a red hat, and a white shirt with red suspenders was throwing items into a cart half-filled with loaves of bread. His back was to us, so I couldn't see his face, but he looked suspiciously like a gnome. He was pushing the cart with one hand and grabbing items off the shelves with the other. I froze, gesturing to the man with a lift of my chin. "That's not your elemental, is it?" When she said nothing, I pressed on. "What's he doing?"

"It looks to me like he's having trouble making up his mind," she said. "Let's just give him a minute and see if it works itself out."

"I don't know, Envy. That doesn't look like indecision. That looks like mindless shopping. Like your elemental has an impulse problem."

Envy snapped her fingers and smiled brightly as she guided me away from the bread in aisle 7. "Impulse problem. That's a perfect segue, Pride. Did you give Lust that tiara as a token of your feelings, or do you just have an impulse problem?"

"Neither," I growled. "I bought Lust that tiara because I wanted her to have it. It's really as simple as that."

Envy huffed, peering at me quizzically. "There has to be more to it than that, Pride. You wanted her to have it, sure. But I want a Lamborghini. When should I expect that in the driveway?"

"That's a ridiculous question," I said matter-of-factly. "I can't afford a Lamborghini." *And I don't care about you getting what you want*, I thought, but I didn't say that. It would have been rude.

"Of course it's ridiculous. But it makes my point. You didn't just buy it because she wanted it. Heck, you didn't buy it because she wanted it *and* you could afford it. But I'm not sure why you *did* buy it. Was it for ratings? Or do you have feelings for her, despite your protestations about the girlfriend you claim you want back?"

I was working myself into a temper (*How dare she! Who does she think she is?*) when a voice over the loudspeaker announced in rising panic, "Cleanup on aisle 7. Cleanup and a manager to aisle 7!"

Envy and I turned to face each other, both of our eyes wide. We had just passed aisle 7. Without even needing to look, I had a sinking feeling I knew exactly what was happening.

We left the cart where it was and darted back to aisle 7, where, sure enough, the small man was throwing things into an overflowing cart. The pile of bread and bread-related items was towering out of the cart. Each loaf he tried to throw onto the pile bounced off onto the floor. And worse, the elemental was no longer choosing items one by one. He was grabbing armloads of bread, hurling them at the cart without looking.

The floor was covered with bread. And the mess was growing.

"Oh no, not again," Envy breathed. She raced toward the elemental, grabbing him by the suspenders from behind. "Elemental!" she hissed, trying to sound menacing while keeping her voice low to prevent a scene. "Elemental, you stop that *right now!*"

The elemental ignored her completely, reaching with its stubby fingers for a package of tortillas. Up ahead, someone gasped, shouting, "Young lady, you get your hands off that child this *instant!*" She was holding her phone up at arm's length. I couldn't tell if she was preparing to call the cops or making a video she hoped might go viral.

Envy looked up and snarled, "He's not a child. He's a gnome! And he's utterly out of control!"

The woman with the phone closed the distance between them, shaking her phone in Envy's face. "I don't know where you grew up, young lady. But in *Odyssey*, we don't make fun of people's disabilities! I'm sorry I called him a child, but he's certainly no gnome! That's a little person, and you need to get your hands *off!*"

"For somebody so worried about his rights, you sure are talking *about* him rather than *to* him!" Envy shot back.

The woman with the phone blanched, dropping the phone to her side. Her gaze shifted from Envy's face to the elemental she clutched by the suspenders. It was still trying to reach the loaves of bread. "I'm sorry," the woman said. "I didn't mean to——"

The elemental grabbed the woman's phone right out of her hand and threw it to the ground, where it shattered. Envy was so surprised that she let go of his suspenders, and the elemental went back to his madcap frenzy. But now, instead of carrying items off the shelves, he began sweeping them to the ground. Within seconds, he'd laid an entire shelf bare.

The shopping woman looked up at Envy with a steely gaze. "You need to get your friend under control," she snapped. Then, throwing her head back, she shouted, *"Can we please get security on aisle 7?"*

# fifteen

. . .

We arrived home much later, exhausted, embarrassed, and bedraggled. The woman with the phone turned out to be a loud-mouth pet salon owner with a community newsletter and a penchant for armchair psychology. While Envy tried to get her elemental under control, the woman kept yammering about the importance of personal responsibility. "You have to own your mistakes," she said haughtily, nose tipped toward the ceiling as Envy tried desperately to constrain the gnome. "When you bring mentally handicapped people to the grocery store, you must be prepared for them to act out. I've written about this *extensively* in my newsletter."

The manager on duty called the cops. By the time they arrived, however, the gnome had despawned, leaving a tortured Envy to explain what had happened without actually explaining what happened. (You try telling the cops you summoned an earth elemental to help with the grocery shopping and see how well it goes over.)

After we put away the groceries, I trudged upstairs to my room. I had fantasies of a long nap and maybe a bubble bath later. But as I was passing by Wrath's room, his door open, something nabbed my attention.

Whispering.

I know that's not enough reason to invade a person's privacy, but—call it intuition. I knew something was up. So I pushed the door open and stepped inside to find Wrath and Sloth huddled together on Wrath's bed, hunched over an open laptop.

A laptop I recognized.

"What are you guys doing?" I asked.

Sloth slammed the laptop closed, her mouth working, looking for words but not finding any. Wrath glared up at me, ready to excoriate me for coming into his room without an invitation. But then his face sagged, and he deflated. "Look, you said you didn't want to be involved anymore. So we didn't involve you anymore."

"That's Walt's laptop, isn't it?" I asked.

Sloth's face was pink, and she wouldn't meet my eyes when she whispered, "Yeah."

"You said you were taking the computer to the cops," I said. "You *know* it's not safe with us. What if whoever killed Eleanor figures out where it is? Do you really want them coming to Sinful House? You're putting everyone at risk!"

"No one knows we have it, Pride," Sloth said, finally meeting my gaze. "The cameras weren't with me when I picked it up."

"Maybe not, but it won't take a genius to track down Eleanor's associates. Geez, Sloth, you were on TV helping her find her missing son!"

"That doesn't mean she'd give me his laptop," Sloth objected. "For all anyone knows, the police already have it."

"Sloth—"

"We haven't found anything so far," Wrath interrupted, his scowl etched deep into his face. "But there has to be something here or else those goons wouldn't have wanted it so bad. But we can't find it. You know what that means, Pride? If *I* can't find it, even with my technopathy?"

I shrugged. "What?"

"It means maybe there's more to this laptop than meets the eye. What if I can't find it because this piece of junk's enchanted?"

I stared down at the computer, brow furrowed. "Enchanted? Is that even possible?"

"How should I know?" Wrath spat, leaning his head back in frustration. "But if it is, we gotta find someone who can detect things like that. See if they can find something we can't."

I threw my housemates a dubious look. "Guys, that just seems…unlikely. If there was an enchantment on the laptop, wouldn't it hide the emails and the website and everything? Maybe there's nothing more to find. Or maybe whatever's on it is so obvious, you've overlooked it."

"That's just it, though," Sloth said with a sigh. "There's like…*nothing* on here. No photographs, no porn, no half-written novels, no nothing. It's *suspiciously* empty."

I shrugged, thrusting my hands into my pockets. "Maybe Walt was a Luddite," I said. "He didn't have any tech in his room. No game systems. No Alexa. No 3D printer. So maybe there's nothing to find because there's *nothing to find*."

Sloth and Wrath shared a look I couldn't read. When Sloth looked back at me, she was frowning. "I want to send the laptop to this woman I know back home. She has psychometry—she can touch objects and sense things about them. She'll be able to tell us if anybody…you know. Messed with it."

"And what if they did?" I challenged. "Then what? Can this woman also erase hypothetical computer enchantments? Can she illuminate secret information we're too inept to locate?"

Sloth's face fell. "Well, no. But—"

"So you want to involve even more people in this when we still don't really know what we're dealing with? And even then, it won't really get us anywhere?"

Gingerly, Wrath slid the laptop off Sloth's lap and, to my surprise, handed it to me. When she saw what he was doing, Sloth shot up straight, eyes wide with objection. "Hang on, what are you—?"

"Pride's right," Wrath said, raising his voice just enough to drown out Sloth's protest. "We tried, Sloth. But whatever is on that laptop isn't for us to find. We've done the best we can. We need to turn this over to the cops and hope they can do a better job." At Sloth's crumpled face, he added. "It's too dangerous."

She nodded mutely and wiped at her nose. I tucked the laptop under my arm. "I'll take it to the station," I promised. "And I'll let Eleanor know. She wouldn't want to put us in harm's way, Sloth. I know she wouldn't."

Sloth slid off Wrath's bed and slipped past me into the hallway. When she was gone, I lifted a hand in a limp wave. "I'm gonna go have a nap or something," I said. "Thanks for siding with me on the laptop thing."

Wrath nodded. "When you're right, you're right. And you were right. We tried, we failed. Time to let the cops do their jobs. Even if I do think all cops are—"

"See you later, Wrath," I interrupted before going off to my own room, dreams of a nap and a bubble bath dancing in my mind.

---

Two days passed quickly, and the night of Cecil's dinner party arrived. Victoria came to the house early to help set up. The rest of us ran around like chickens with our heads cut off, making sure everything was in place. Even the cameramen were helpful for a change. I got the feeling they'd gotten an earful from the network about making this confrontation as successful and dramatic as possible. So instead of being surly and annoying, they pitched in, rearranging furniture and setting up the scene.

Sinful House was teeming with cameras, but most of them weren't hidden. The camera guys and Envy worked together to hide or remove cameras that were out in the open—all the better to catch Cecil off-guard.

Victoria came up with the brilliant idea of assigned seats at dinner, so we'd know how to light the room to best capture Cecil's charade on camera.

The tricky part would be getting Cecil—Jace Thornburgh—to sign a release so the network could air the episode with him in it. But although it might cost the network a pretty penny, our producer, Tricia, assured us they'd worked with guys like him before. There was little Jace Thornburgh wouldn't do for money.

That's why we were in this predicament in the first place.

While the rest of us worked to set the stage, Gluttony prepared a meal fit for a king. He baked two different lasagnas—one with a mouthwatering combination of veal, pork sausage, and beef, the other with eggplant and mushrooms. In addition, he prepared three salads, several loaves of bread, rosemary butter, and home-churned lemon sorbet for dessert. The spread was beautiful. You had to hand it to Gluttony. The guy really knew how to create a five-star experience.

Greed sauntered into the dining room, his hands tucked casually in his pockets. After all my time at Sinful House, I still didn't know Greed well. He kept to himself, and even during our network-mandated house meals, he said little. Tonight wasn't much different. As he took in the spread, all he said was, "You went to a lot of trouble."

"I didn't," I corrected. "Gluttony did. He made all this himself. He saved our hides, really. None of this would be possible without him."

Greed offered a slight nod, still surveying the table. "I hope it goes well."

I paused. "Are you coming to dinner?"

Now, the barest shadow of a smile crept over his lips. "Wouldn't miss it. Though I'll be sure to keep strictly to the wine. It's store-bought, yes?"

I chuckled. "The wine is safe. But wine on an empty stomach?"

Greed smiled for real now. "Can't be worse than what you've got planned. And I like my secrets."

He said nothing more as he sauntered out the way he'd come in.

Curtain was in half an hour, and one by one, the housemates started trickling into the common rooms. Everyone was dolled up in their Sunday best. But of course, Lust put everyone else to shame. She was wearing the tiara we bought at the citywide garage sale. I couldn't decide if she looked majestic or insane and eventually settled on a combination of the two. Either way, I couldn't keep my eyes off her. Besides the crown, she wore a black dress that looked like she'd been poured into it. When she saw me staring, she blushed a bright crimson. I returned that blush and tore my eyes away, my pulse pounding in my ears.

As the housemates poured wine and Gluttony passed around hors d'oeuvres, Bailey Preston arrived. I gave her a quick tour of the house and offered her a glass of wine, which she accepted but didn't drink. She kept fidgeting with her jewelry and smoothing her hair into place even though she already looked perfect. She was worrying the rings on her fingers and biting her lip when she placed a hand on my elbow and gave a little squeeze.

"You really went above and beyond for this," she said. "I can't tell you how grateful I am."

I shrugged. "It was the least I could do. Anyway, this was all Victoria's idea. I know Tamora and I will probably never see eye to eye, but I can't stand the idea of someone being preyed upon like that. Everyone deserves to be with someone who loves them for who they are and not what they bring to the table."

Bailey nodded, her chin wobbling. "Is Tamora coming tonight?"

I shook my head. "We didn't invite her. I have no idea how this is going to go down, and we don't want to embarrass her. We'll show her the footage, though."

Bailey hrmmed, her lips pinched. "If this is successful and we get Cecil to admit who he really is, I want to arrange a *real* meeting between Tamora and Jeff."

Of all the things she could have said, I wasn't expecting that. "A real meeting?"

Bailey swallowed and fidgeted once again with her hair. "I know I said I didn't believe in the afterlife. And I still don't. Not really. But my sister does. So if we get Cecil on camera admitting how he duped my sister—and believe me, I can't wait to hear the details on that—it's going to destroy her. The only thing that'll help her heal is speaking with Jeff. The *real* Jeff. I think she needs to hear from him one more time."

Her request made a bitter sense. One day in the (probably far) future, Tamora would not only forgive us but be grateful we saved her from the nightmare of a fraudulent marriage. But in the short term, Bailey was right. Tamora would hate all of us when the truth came out. I didn't care about that, but of course, her sister did. Tamora might even slip into a depression like she had before. I cared somewhat more about that. I'd been depressed before. It's not fun. I wouldn't wish it on anyone.

However, I wasn't sure what I was supposed to do about any of this.

"I see ghosts," I admitted. "But I see them here on earth. Among the living. I can't cross over to the other side and find people. I'm not a medium."

"You're not," Bailey agreed, "but we both know someone who is."

I opened my mouth to ask for more details when Victoria bustled into the room. "Come on, you two. We have a show to put on. It's time to go catch a predator."

# sixteen

. . .

At 7 p.m., the doorbell rang.

Everyone took their places, and I went to the door, my heart thumping in my throat. I didn't know why I was nervous. But I don't generally like surprises, and there was no telling how this would all pan out.

I tried to be prepared for anything. I braced myself for the man on the porch to be a stranger. I prepared for it to be a woman. I'd seen the MTV show *Catfish*. When it came to deception, human ingenuity knew no bounds. The person outside could be *anyone*.

With a breath to steady my nerves, I pulled the door open.

I blinked. Standing on the porch was Jace Thornburgh—the same man I'd seen in the Facebook photos and the startup articles online.

Kind of.

The pictures we'd found of Jace Thornburgh were of a good-looking middle-aged guy who drank dry martinis in polos and khakis and Docksider slip-ons. But this guy looked nothing like that. He was wearing a long white linen tunic over a loose pair of maroon linen trousers. He wore suede Birkenstocks revealing recently manicured toes. Around his left wrist, he wore a bracelet of milky jade mala beads. His wavy brown hair was growing out, almost touching his shoulders. Small gold hoops adorned both earlobes.

In short, he looked like a cross between Mahatma Gandhi and Jesus. Not a bad look if you're pretending to be a medium.

Finally, I found my voice. "Jeff?" I asked.

The man blinked and then smiled warmly. "Cecil," he corrected. "Understandable mistake."

I didn't know what to say. His voice sounded nothing like the man Victoria had spoken to on the phone. We stared at each other a moment before he cleared his throat and asked, "May I come in?"

I stepped aside and led him to the living room where everyone was seated. "I can't thank you enough for showing up," I said. "I hope you don't mind, but I've invited a few friends over to join us for dinner. Victoria you already know." At her name, Victoria nodded, smiling prettily. "And this is Bailey Preston, Tamora's sister. But maybe you already know that."

Cecil shook his head. "I'm afraid I don't. It's nice to meet you," he said, directing this comment at both Bailey and Victoria.

"The others are some of Tamora's more recent acquaintances. I figure if we're going to make this work—"

"Let me interrupt you," he said. He drew his hands

to his chest, holding them in a prayerful position. "I know when you and Jace spoke on the phone, you had a lot of questions. It seems you may believe I'm here for… dubious purposes." He smiled awkwardly, fingers worrying the mala beads at his wrist. "But whatever you may think of me, I assure you I am who I say I am. My name is Cecil Bradshaw, and I'm a psychic medium. I channeled the spirit of Jeff Bishop into my body, where he continues to reside. Usually, I'm myself. But with just a little nudge in the right direction, Jeff comes to the front and takes over this body."

"Neat trick," Greed said, one leg thrown casually over the other. "So you can make this switch on command?"

Cecil hesitated. "I don't know if I'd say it's on command," he admitted. "I'd say more…when the time is right."

Victoria shot Greed a withering look as I escorted our guest to a loveseat where we both sat. Gluttony had set out trays of hors d'oeuvres, including watercress sandwiches and an impressive charcuterie board replete with a half dozen meats, cheeses, and fruits. "Dinner will be ready in just a minute," Victoria said, "But we thought we could begin the evening on a more casual note." Victoria tilted her head to the side. "I'd love to hear more about how—and why—you channeled Jeff into your body."

Cecil reached for a sandwich and popped it into his mouth. He brushed his hands together and crossed his legs as he leaned back into the sofa cushions. "Of course. Well, where do I begin? As a spiritual counselor,

I do a lot of this kind of work: séances, automatic writing, past-life regression, things like that. But I'm also a medium. Most of that work is less about the spirit and more about helping grieving people heal. I channel spirits of the dead so their loved ones can move on. I work with families fighting over wills, wives who want to hear that their husbands still love them, things like that. So I was surprised when the person who came to me for medium services was not a friend or family member. It was a business associate of Jeff Bishop's. A man named Jace Thornburgh."

I gawped, my eyes going wide. *Wait, what? He* was Jace Thornburgh. I'd seen proof with my own eyes. I saw his Facebook profile. I saw his photo on the startup news site. The man sitting before us was a milquetoast guru, sure, but *he was Jace Thornburgh!*

Wasn't he?

I opened my mouth to state the obvious when Gluttony burst into the room, hands on his hips. "Dinner's on the table," he said. "Y'all best get in there before the food gets cold. I didn't spend all that time in the kitchen to let my hard work go to waste."

We knew better than to defy Gluttony, so we all climbed to our feet. As we headed into the dining room, I sidled up next to Sloth and whispered in her ear. "Well? What do you make of this? Is he telling the truth?"

Sloth's expression was serene. "It's super weird," she said, reaching for a pigtail to chew on. "I can't tell you if he's telling the truth. I tried to read his mind, but there was so much noise in there. Not normal noise, either. He wasn't just jumping from thought to thought like people do. It was like multiple conversations were happening at once, everyone talking on top of each other. I couldn't hear his thoughts over the conversations."

I quirked an eyebrow in surprise. "Have you heard anything like that before?"

Sloth shook her head. "No, not like that. Some people play noise in their heads to keep out intrusive thoughts. Like, a guy I know back home repeats lines from movies and song lyrics over and over again, so he doesn't have to hear himself think. But this was…different. I don't know what to make of it."

I sighed. "Well, don't worry about it too much. Between your mind reading and Gluttony's special dinner, I have a feeling we'll have our answers soon enough."

We took our seats around the table with Cecil at the head. As usual, Gluttony's feast was outstanding. Victoria acted as the hostess, preparing plates and passing them down the table. No one touched their food until everyone was served. Finally, when the last person had their dish in front of them, I turned to face Cecil.

"We asked Gluttony to prepare a special meal tonight," I said. "He's the best cook in the house. I hope you're hungry."

At the other end of the table, Victoria began pouring wine. As I pretended to cut into my lasagna, I watched Cecil from the corner of my eye. He took a huge bite, and ecstasy washed over his face as he chewed, his eyes rolling to the back of his head. "Oh my word," he exclaimed through a full mouth. "This is fantastic. Why aren't the rest of you as big as a house? If I lived here and I got to eat like this every day, you'd have to roll me out the front door."

We chuckled politely, but tensions were high. Cecil had already eaten several mouthfuls before the rest of us tentatively took small bites of the dinner. After all, we knew what was in the food.

After a few minutes of quiet chewing, Wrath said, "Since nobody else has the chops to say anything, I guess I'll do it. We've all seen Jace Thornburgh's photos, man. Unless he has a secret twin, you're him. I mean, you're obviously Jace Thornburgh, not Cecil Bradshaw or whatever. So why are you pretending…"

But Wrath didn't have a chance to complete the question. In the middle of his sentence, Wrath's words stuttered to a stop as he balked, eyes blinking rapidly as he stared at the other end of the table.

Confused, I turned to Cecil. It took a moment, but suddenly, I realized why Wrath had been shocked into silence.

Cecil changed right before my eyes.

One minute, he was a jovial, charming man with a casual command of the room. But now, he was scowling, brow wrinkled in confusion as he dropped his fork, which clattered to the floor. He pulled his hands away from the table and pushed up his sleeves until they revealed the mala beads at his wrists. Then, his head fell backward, and he sighed heavily. "Cecil again," he breathed, his voice low. "Why am I at Cecil's dinner party?"

The room went silent. The man speaking was not

Cecil, but I recognized this voice. I'd heard this voice on the phone in the Crypt.

The voice belonged to Jace Thornburgh.

The change was not dramatic, but it was noticeable. Cecil's voice was flowy and warm like he was trying to put you to sleep. This voice was sharper and louder, like he wanted you to sit up and pay attention.

But it wasn't just the voice that was different. His body language changed, his vibes palpably less relaxed. His shoulders were tighter; his jaw was clenched. Where Cecil had been open and welcoming, this man was guarded, like one of us might attack him at any moment.

He dropped his head into his hands, fingers buried deep in the roots of his hair. When he looked up, his expression was stern. "I agreed to let Cecil bring me here," he said. "But we agreed he'd stay until we got home. So…I'm not sure why I'm here and Cecil's not."

I stared, unable to reply. Did he think *we* had any answers? I was grasping for a way to respond when at the other end of the table, Greed inexplicably asked, "Who are we speaking to now?"

My head swiveled to face Greed. His eyes were trained on Cecil, and his expression was tender but professional, like a professor addressing a nervous first-year student.

I swiveled my head again to look at Cecil. I was beginning to feel like I was at a tennis match.

The man snorted out a heavy sigh. "Jace," he said. "My name is Jace Thornburgh."

I glanced over at Greed. He was leaning forward

onto his elbows, his chin resting atop laced fingers. He was still wearing that eerie professor look. Frankly, it was the most of Greed's personality I'd ever seen, and it was creeping me out. He cleared his throat and asked, "Jace, are you the host?"

The man nodded. "Yes. You'd think I'd be used to this by now. But I guess you never really get used to it."

I was staring so intently at Cecil and trying to make sense of what I'd just seen that I almost jumped out of my skin when Wrath demanded, "What the heck is going on? Cecil?"

Greed smiled at Cecil(?) Jace(?) and dropped him a wink. "I can explain it," Greed said. It wasn't an offer to us, however. It felt like an olive branch to Jace. "But it is *you* we are speaking of, so perhaps you'd like to speak for yourself?" He softened his voice even further and said, "It's entirely up to you. *Jace.*" He put a subtle but unmistakable emphasis on the man's name.

Jace—look, even I could take the hint—looked like he'd rather be anywhere else on earth than sitting at this table with us. His skin had gone ashen, and his jowls sagged. "I, uh." He cleared his throat and looked down into his lap. "I have a psychological condition called dissociative identity disorder."

I chanced a look around the table. I had absolutely no idea what he was talking about, but no way would I admit as much. Thankfully, my housemates—all except Greed—looked just as perplexed as I felt. Greed made an encouraging motion at Jace, who sucked in a breath and tried again.

"It used to be called multiple personality disorder?"

I sank back into my chair, my hand covering my mouth in surprise. Oh. I'd heard of this condition, but only on TV shows and that one Sally Field movie. The man sitting at the head of the table had come to us as Cecil, an easygoing spiritual guru. But he wasn't Cecil now. Cecil had left the building.

This man was Jace Thornburgh.

Again, Jace shifted in his seat and continued. "I was diagnosed as a teenager," he said. "I don't know any of you, so sorry if I don't feel like giving you my entire medical history. But you invited *Cecil* to dinner, not me, so I guess I owe you an explanation of why I'm here, and Cecil isn't. But unfortunately, I don't have a great answer to that."

"Actually," Greed interrupted, "it is *we* who owe *you* an explanation." He gestured at the feast in front of us. "We tricked Cecil. Gluttony is a kitchen witch. He enchanted tonight's dinner with magic that makes people tell the truth. It's why we were hesitant to begin eating and why I'm confessing this now." He grinned and winked again. "I can't say for sure, but I suspect that's why you emerged when Cecil ate our food. You are the original personality, after all. Your body's true north. The magic forced the switch."

"I see," Jace said, voice low. "Well, under the circumstances, I'm gonna choose not to be ticked off. I assume you want to know how and why Jeff got stuck in Cecil's—and my—body."

"Or *if,*" Victoria clarified, her voice icy.

"*If* isn't the question," Jace said, shaking his head.

"That really did happen. And it's all my fault. Good grief, I hardly even know where to begin."

Envy was watching all this with rapt attention. "Begin at the beginning," she advised. "And when you come to the end, stop."

Jace grinned nervously. "Well, I can tell you what I know. I met Jeff on an Everest expedition. He sort of became my climbing buddy, I guess you'd say. When you go through something like that, even with a complete stranger, you form a bond with them. There were lots of other people on the expedition, of course. But I was attracted to Jeff not just because he was famous, but also because he was more like me than the others."

"More like you how?" Bailey asked.

"Uh, well…lots of the other guys were survivalists. They had Everest on their bucket lists, you know, so they were there to, like, prove something. Adrenaline junkies. But Jeff and I were different. We weren't there because we got off on the rush of danger. We were there trying to find ourselves. I know how that sounds," he scoffed. "But it's true. I like to think we would have become friends if we'd both survived."

I chanced another look around the table. All my housemates were as transfixed as I was. I guess it's not every day you meet someone with multiple personalities living inside one body.

"Jeff got sick in what they call the *death zone*. There's not much oxygen up there, and you're supposed to pass through that zone quickly. But the problem is, our expedition was overbooked. Imagine that. You finally get out of the hectic rush of day-to-day life only to stand in a queue to reach the top of Everest because the expedition was *overbooked*." He laughed again, a dry, mirthless sound. "Anyway, it's not uncommon for people to get sick in the death zone. That's why they call it the death zone. Jeff started hallucinating. He was talking to people who weren't there. Mostly, he spoke to Tamora, who I guess was his wife."

I shot a look at Bailey, but her expression was unreadable. She was watching Jace with as steely a gaze as I'd ever seen.

"He talked about private things that happened between them. Dinners they'd shared, jokes, TV shows. Stupid stuff like that. I tried to be there for him. But he was deteriorating fast, and—"

He sat up straight, his mouth drawn into a hard line. "I don't want to talk about Jeff's death," he said. "All I'll say is this. In my final moments with him, he was delirious. The last person he mentioned was someone called Tori."

It took everything I had not to look at Victoria to gauge her reaction. After all, Tori was her secret, and I wouldn't be the one to expose her. Instead, I asked, "Who's Tori?"

"I don't know," Jace admitted with a shrug. "He just kept saying he was sorry. He passed away before revealing the last of his secrets."

A collective sigh went around the table, and the energy shifted. It's always hard to talk intimately about death, even the death of a stranger. Humans have a tremendous capacity for empathy when we allow ourselves to feel it.

"Anyway, that's the backstory. When I got back state-side, it took me a while to acclimate to daily life, you know? Everest kicked my butt, and I watched someone die. It changed me. But after a while, I realized I needed to talk to Jeff. Not just about business, but about our experience. So I did something out of character. I asked Cecil for help."

"How?" Sloth asked. "I mean, I hope this isn't an ignorant question. But, if you and Cecil are the same person, then…?"

"I'm sorry, Sloth, but I must interrupt." Greed was leaning forward and craning his neck to address Sloth directly, who sat on the same side of the table as he did. "Cecil and Jace are *not* the same person. Or at least, not the same personality. They merely reside in the same body."

Jace was silent a moment. Finally, he looked to Greed and said, "You seem to know a bit about this. Are you a doctor or something?"

Greed's lips tightened into something like a smile. "I'm a psychiatrist," he said.

If you'd told me Greed was some kind of rock band dropout or a vampire cosplayer, I would have believed you. That's the kind of energy Greed gives off.

Never in a million years would I have guessed that guy to be a *psychiatrist*. I immediately felt terrible for his patients.

Greed shifted in his seat and said, "Dissociative iden-tity disorder means there are several personalities—we call these *alters*—living inside the host. They can converse among themselves. Of course, psychiatry doesn't *really* understand how that happens. For as much as we like to think otherwise, the brain is still the great unknown. We know far less about how it works than we pretend."

"I guess that explains it," Sloth said almost to herself. She glanced over to Jace. "I'm a mind reader. My job tonight was to listen to your thoughts—sorry, *Cecil's* thoughts—to see if he was telling the truth. But when I tried, I heard so many other voices. I couldn't make out one from another. It was just so much chatter and noise."

Greed nodded. "You heard the alters having conversations. That's interesting. I'd like to talk to you more about that at another time." He adjusted his gaze to settle once again on Jace. "How many alters do you have?"

"Five that we know of," he mumbled.

No one knew what to say to that. It seemed intrusive and rude to ask more about the alters (even though I, for one, was dying to know more.) After a protracted silence, Wrath finally said, "So I guess I have to be the one to ask. *Again.*" He gave me a dirty look as he said this. "Can we talk to Jeff? I mean, can he come out to play?"

I threw Wrath a disgusted look, but he just shrugged and made bug eyes at me like he had done nothing wrong. I looked back at Jace, who was smiling. If he was offended by Wrath's question or tone, he didn't show it. "I wish I could help you there," he said. "But I don't have anything to do with Jeff. Not in his current state, anyway. That's all Cecil. And I can't *make*

Cecil come out. That's not how this works. At least, not for me."

Without meaning to, I looked to Greed for confirmation. My housemate nodded sagely. "Some people claim they can switch alters at will," he explained. "But in my limited experience, most people can't. The alters come out when they are needed." Greed looked at Jace, his eyes narrowing as he tilted his head to the side questioningly. "What makes Cecil come out?"

Jace cleared his throat and adjusted in his seat. "According to my doctor, Cecil is an internal soother. He comes out when I feel stressed or I'm in a new, uncomfortable situation. His presence is very calming. Or so I'm told. When I deal with him behind the scenes, I don't find him calming. Mostly I just find him annoying." He grinned as he said this, color rising in his cheeks. "But he's useful."

"If he comes out when you're stressed, how come he didn't show up on Mount Everest?" Sloth asked, leaning forward eagerly in her seat. "Or did he?"

"That's a good question," Jace conceded. "The best I can guess is that Cecil couldn't have survived Everest. I was the one who trained, not him. My alters don't share their skill sets. Cecil can channel spirits and meditate and all that jazz—I can't. But similarly, I have what it takes to climb and survive Everest. I don't think Cecil would have made it out of basecamp."

The group was quiet for a long time, our dinner forgotten. Suddenly, Jace was on his feet, rubbing his palms on Cecil's white tunic. "I'm feeling a little on display," he admitted. "Especially sitting here wearing

Cecil's clothes. Anyone mind if we pause this whole thing? I need a minute."

Jace didn't need our permission, of course, and he didn't wait for it. He bolted out of the dining room and disappeared around the corner. In the distance, a door opened and then slammed shut.

All eyes turned to Greed. He was leaning back in his chair now, and without Jace present, his relaxed, professional demeanor vanished. Now he looked like the Greed I was used to—wolfish and predatory. "I've never seen that happen in the wild like that," he said. "I've only treated a handful of patients with DID. Definitely never met anyone who channeled a spirit into their body. Can you imagine the papers I could publish about this? I've got to get Jace to sign a release form."

Lust growled, throwing Greed a disgusted look. "That poor man is suffering, and you're thinking about your career?"

"Not at all," Greed shot back. "I'm thinking about the *money*."

"You're disgusting."

"I'm honest," he quipped. "This could lead to book deals, movie rights, the whole shebang."

"That's so wrong, man," Wrath put in, sneering and shaking his head. "The poor dude's got an emotionally vapid millionaire stuck inside him, and all you care about is dollar signs. That's the trouble with our whole society! Capitalism is the death of humanity, man, I'm telling you!" He banged a hand on the table. "Greed is the perfect example of why this country is deteriorating! Our crumbling morals, our disregard for fellow man! Capitalism will destroy us from the inside out!"

I sighed and gave Wrath a weary look. "Now's not the time, Wrath."

"It's never the time!" he shouted. "But in actuality, it's *always* the time! When better to illuminate our system's flaws than when we're staring in the face of someone broken by it?"

"Stop it," I said, my voice taking on a threatening edge. "We just met this guy. You can't call him broken. It's not right."

"He's a mental case, man," Wrath said, shaking his head in despair. "But it's not his fault. He's a reflection of each of us, torn to pieces by an evil society."

"I have a question." We turned our heads to Sloth, who was chewing on a pigtail and dipping a finger into her red sauce. "If Cecil and Jeff conspired to marry Tamora together, what was the plan for when Cecil wasn't in charge of the body? Do Jace or any of the alters have girlfriends or boyfriends of their own?"

"Good question," I said. "But we won't get any answers unless we get Cecil to come out. But I don't know how to do that, and I don't want to pester Jace. Cecil agreed to this interrogation. Jace didn't."

"Technically, Jace agreed *for* Cecil," Victoria reminded me.

I ignored her.

Gluttony stood up and began cleaning the table. "All this work for nothing," he muttered. "That's okay, though. I love lasagna. Even if it does make you tell the truth against your will. I'm gonna eat me some and hide out in my room where nobody can bother me. The rest of y'all are invited to do the same."

One by one, my housemates and I got up and cleared our places. Eating the lasagna in private was a good idea, so I wrapped up my food and placed it on the counter for later. First, I needed to go talk to Jace.

It took a while, but eventually, I found him down on the beach. He was sitting on the shore, his bare toes buried in the sand. He didn't tear his gaze away from the ocean as I settled down beside him. We shared a long, quiet moment with only the crash of the waves for company. The sun had already dipped below the horizon, and a cool breeze made my skin pimple over.

Without looking at me, Jace said, "I'm sorry about all this."

I shrugged, following Jace's gaze out over the ocean. I didn't have dissociative identity disorder, but my brain wasn't exactly normal, either. I struggled with anxiety, the inability to read social cues, reckless pride, and myriad other things. So I guess you could say I knew a thing or two about imbalanced mental health. "It's not your fault," I said. "I want to say we were trying to help a friend, but that's a lie. We were trying to win a contest for a TV show. But obviously, we had no idea what was really going on. If we'd known it would lead to this…"

I let my voice trail off. I wanted to believe I would have respected Jace's privacy, trading in my win for his wellbeing. But at that moment, I didn't know if it was true, so Gluttony's lasagna prevented me from saying it.

Let me tell you, that made me feel like trash.

"At least you're handling it well," he said. "Lots of people write me off as a lunatic."

"I see ghosts," I said. "So I know what that's like."

"Ghosts, huh?" He chuckled. "That's cool. Or maybe it's not. That's not normal, so. Maybe you should see a shrink."

"I do. Well, I used to. Not for the ghosts, though. For other stuff. I should probably make an appointment," I added, knowing I wouldn't.

Jace smiled. "I was just kidding."

"Oh."

Jace was quiet for a moment. Then he said, "What will you do if Cecil doesn't come out?"

"Nothing, I guess. It'll be up to Tamora at that point." I paused. "Well, hang on. How long are you staying?"

"I don't even remember getting here," he reminded me. "So I have no idea what the itinerary is." He dug a hand into a pocket and retrieved a phone. "This is Cecil's phone. We each have our own. I don't even know the passwords to some of them. But I know Cecil's." After flipping to the correct app, he said, "Looks like I'm leaving tomorrow evening."

I leaned back into my palms, the sand under my hands shifting with my weight. I grinned. "Well, in that case, we might be in luck. I think I know someone who can help."

# seventeen

. . .

"I had begun to think I wouldn't hear from you again," Andromeda said. "And here you are, gracing me with the glory of your voice before I've even had my coffee."

I smiled into the phone, abashed. It was early in the morning—too early for a phone call. But after the previous night's shenanigans, it couldn't wait. "I didn't plan to call you," I admitted, "but we could use your help. Are you still in town?"

"I am," she confirmed.

"Great. Well, listen. If you're still in the mood to do a favor for Tamora, I've got an idea."

I told her my plan and was not at all surprised when Andromeda readily agreed. She'd grown up with Tamora, after all. She was a good friend and wanted to help.

"I don't know much about dissociative identity disorder," Andromeda said, "but this seems like a good plan to me. And Tamora agreed to this?"

I sighed, digging my free hand into my pocket. "I haven't talked to her yet, but Bailey is confident we can convince her."

"I hope you can," she said. "This will go better for all of us if she doesn't fight it. Good luck. You'll need it."

I disconnected and then called Bailey.

"Andromeda says she'll do it," I said. "Now we've just got to convince your sister."

"I'll convince her," she said. "Leave that to me. I'll meet you at Tamora's in thirty minutes. Have faith, Pride! We've got this!"

I disconnected without saying goodbye. Faith was something I lacked in spades.

When Bailey and I arrived at Tamora's house half an hour later, I was nervous. I didn't know why. I stood behind as Bailey rang the doorbell.

The door creaked open, and an exasperated Tamora deflated when she saw us. "What are you doing here?"

"Good morning to you, too," Bailey said, a forced cheerfulness in her voice. "I'm here to update you on what's going on. Can we come in?"

Tamora shook her head. "No."

"Fine." Bailey sighed and popped her hands on her hips. "We want you to host another séance."

Now, Tamora's eyes narrowed. "Another séance? What for?"

Bailey hesitated. "Tammy, there's something you should know. He's here in Odyssey. Cecil. And Jeff's with him. With your help, we can bring Jeff out and maybe release him from Cecil's body."

Tamora glanced from her sister to me and back again. "He's here in Odyssey? Why didn't you tell me? Why am I just hearing about this *now?*"

"We had to make sure it was really him," Bailey explained. "We had to protect you. But now you need to know. If this goes right, it'll be your last chance to talk to Jeff. With any luck, after today, Jeff won't be trapped anymore."

Tamora glared at her sister long and hard before directing her ire at me. "How do I know you're not just trying to get me back for setting you up?"

I shrugged. "Holding grudges is a waste of energy. But if you don't believe that, look at it this way: I want to be likable on TV. Doing something mean to a widow seems like a fast-track to becoming Public Enemy Number One."

She pursed her lips, considering. Then, she rolled her eyes and threw up her hands. "Whatever. Do what you need to do, Bailey."

"I'm doing this for you, Tammy."

"If you were really doing this for me, you'd let me marry Jeff and get out of my business."

"Fine," Bailey said. "Then I'm doing it for you *and* Jeff. You can't just let him stay locked up in someone else's body, Tammy. Even you have to see how messed up that is."

Tamora didn't reply to this. Instead, she opened the door wider and stepped aside, bidding us entry. She gestured upstairs toward the library. "Guess you better get to work," she said. "I have other things to do."

Tamora disappeared around a corner as Bailey and I

climbed the steps. "The séance begins in an hour!" Bailey shouted.

She turned to me, eyes wide. "That went better than I hoped." She gestured toward the library. "We haven't got a lot of time. Let's get moving."

———

An hour later, we were standing in Tamora's library with the rest of the guests we'd assembled. There were more people here today than at the last séance: Bailey, Tamora, and Victoria were present, along with Andromeda at the head of the table and all the housemates except Sloth. For my plan to work, we needed to keep Jace in the dark. Sloth was the designated babysitter, entertaining Jace downstairs while the rest of us set up for the big show.

The room felt stuffy and claustrophobic as we found our places around the table. It was a warm day, and the heat from the candles only added to the discomfort. It was also weird having a séance in the middle of the morning. Although Bailey had drawn the curtains, scant sunlight filtered through the windows. Birds chirped outside. The smells of Tamora's breakfast, fried bacon and coffee, drifted in from downstairs. The smells of breakfast muddled with Tamora's overpowering perfume and the scent of burning candles made me queasy.

There was a knock at the door. "Come in," Bailey said.

The door opened, and Sloth poked in her head. "You ready for us?"

Bailey nodded. "Perfect timing. Come on in."

Sloth pushed the door open wide and guided in a blindfolded Jace. He was dressed in Cecil's clothes: a navy-blue tunic and matching pants. I guess Cecil hadn't packed anything normal. He had pulled his hair into a ponytail and removed the gold earrings and mala bracelets from yesterday. He shuffled into the room with baby steps as Sloth guided him with her hand at the small of his back.

I watched Tamora's face as Jace stumbled toward his seat across from her. She'd never seen the man before her now, the man she'd agreed to marry. Jace was a good-looking guy, but he was no Israeli model. Her eyes followed him through the room, her face carefully blank. I wondered what was going through her head. Was she angry? Did she mind his looks? Was she worried? Confused?

I searched her face and body language for clues but didn't find any. No big surprise there, though. My catalog of Tamora's expressions contained only three entries: "Undeserved hatred for Pride," "Moderately deserved annoyance at Bailey," and "Smug knowledge that she's right about everything."

Once Jace slid into place, Sloth sat next to him, maneuvering herself to within arm's reach of her charge. Jace's face was down-turned, and though I couldn't see his eyes, the shadows cast by the candles made his face look somber. Envy, seated to my left, leaned toward me, her voice low and soft in my ear. "Are we sure this is a good idea?" she asked, her gaze flitting to Jace's face. "It seems, I don't know… cruel."

"He agreed to it," I assured her. "Remember, we blindfolded him so he'll be shocked when he sees where he is. Jace said Cecil comes out when he feels out of his element. I'm hoping this is as out of Jace's element as you can get."

From unseen speakers overhead, a soft but morbid melody drifted into the room. Then Andromeda's voice cut through the darkness. "I've invited you all here today to commune with the dead," she said, her voice heavy and singsong. "It is a most gracious gift the dead offer when they deign to return to the physical realm and share their wisdom with us, and for this, we are grateful. Now, as we attune ourselves to the vibrations of the afterworld, I invite you, Sloth, to remove the blinds that prevent our good man Jace Thornburgh from seeing what he is meant to see."

Gently, Sloth reached over to untie Jace's blindfold. When the cloth dropped away, Jace blinked into the darkness. He took in the candles and the dozens of various crystals adorning the table. His eyes swept over the collection of animal bones, Tarot cards, astrological dice, and assorted daggers. He lifted his eyes slowly to the end of the table where Andromeda sat with her arms on their rests, a coy smile twisted on her lips. Her hair was piled high in a fluffy cloud of pink, held in place with Lust's tiara and dotted with plastic spiders tucked inside her many curls. She wore a black lace dress with long bell sleeves and a deep V neckline. Her lips were painted black, and she wore a velvet choker with a vintage cameo at her throat.

To summarize, she looked ridiculous. She looked nothing like the ethereal goddess her brand made her out to be. She looked like some kind of dollar-store Halloween matriarch, and not in a good way. I'm not even sure there *is* a good way to achieve that look.

(For the record, I had nothing to do with her costume. Andromeda and Lust concocted this cockamamie monstrosity on their own. I argued it would be enough for her to wear her usual attire, but I was outvoted.)

I held my breath, eyes trained on Jace to see if our work here made him uncomfortable enough to nudge him right out of his body.

And what do you know? It worked.

In an instant, Jace's body language changed. Confidence shimmied up his spine, and he sat up straight, his shoulders squaring. Even so, he looked relaxed. A smile broke over his face, and his eyes twinkled in the dim light. He looked around the table and tapped his fingertips together, nodding in silent greeting as he met each person's gaze. "It's good to see you all again," he said finally. "I trust I'm not interrupting anything?"

Tentatively, I asked, "Cecil?"

"In the flesh," he said, flashing us a wide smile. "Well, not exactly *my* flesh, but I assume you take my meaning."

With Cecil's arrival, the mood of the room changed. It no longer felt like we were leading a prisoner to his execution. Now, it felt like a gathering of friends performing crucial spiritual work. Which, if you believe in that sort of thing, was exactly what we were doing.

(I mean, I'm using the words *friends* loosely here, but cut me some slack.)

"I invite you all to link hands," Andromeda instructed. I took Envy's hand in my left, Lust's hand in my right. At the touch of Lust's skin, a thrill ran down my spine. Seriously, one of these days, I just needed to ask her out on a proper date. The tension between us was getting ridiculous.

*Focus*, I reminded myself. Maybe sitting beside Lust hadn't been such a good idea.

"Do you know why we brought you here today, Cecil?" Andromeda asked.

Cecil nodded. "I have my suspicions. I assume you want to manifest Jeff."

Andromeda nodded. "Yes. The end goal today is to draw him out of your body and into my own. And hopefully, by releasing him from your flesh, we will untangle him from the multiples that already thrive within you. And then, when we are done, I will release him to his home on the other side."

Tamora's voice, sharp and icy, cut through the room. "And what if that's not what *I* want?"

All eyes shifted to Tamora. She was clutching Wrath's hand on her left and Bailey's hand on her right as she stared daggers at Andromeda. "Remember what I said? I *specifically* said I didn't want anyone else to channel him. You all promised. You *promised!*"

Andromeda huffed, lifting her chin in small defiance. "We *did* make that promise, Tamora. That was before we understood the extent of this situation. It's not just Jeff trapped within Cecil's vehicle. It's Jace and Cecil and the other alters burdened with a personality that isn't part of their system. We owe it to them to release Jeff. And we owe it to you."

I watched as Tamora's eyes grew soft, damp with tears. "It's not what I want," she whimpered. "Even if most of the time he's not present in that body, I still want to be with him for the few moments I can. Is that so terrible?"

Andromeda was silent for a long stretch. Then she said, "Why don't we ask Jeff what *he* wants, Tamora? Wouldn't that be the right thing to do?"

Our host opened her mouth to speak, and for a moment, I thought she would refuse. But then, reluctantly, Tamora dropped her chin in a tacit nod. "All right," she whispered.

Andromeda cleared her throat and sat up a little straighter. "I invite you all to still your minds and open your hearts to welcome in the dead. As for you, Cecil, I ask that you release hold of your body and allow the universe to work through you in all its miraculous and wondrous ways. You are not merely a son of Adam. You are part and particle of the larger universe. Everything flows through you. You are stardust. You are ephemeral. And so I ask you to vanish and make room for the man we know as Jeff Bishop."

The room was silent and still. I felt Lust's breathing, the warmth rising in her hands. I waited with bated breath for the shenanigans to start. But unlike the first séance, there was no shaking of tables. No books fell from their shelves. Nothing levitated, no one screamed, and windows did not shatter. The only sign that something supernatural was happening was the slight drop in temperature.

I stared at the other end of the table, watching Cecil intently. He closed his eyes and breathed in deeply through his nose. After a while, he opened his eyes. He looked directly at Tamora and began to cry.

"Oh," he whispered, astonishment washing over him as he scrubbed his face with both hands. "Oh, Tam-Tam. It's really you." His voice was hoarse and heavy with the thickness in his throat. "I can't believe it. After all this time. I never thought I'd see that beautiful face again."

Tamora's face crumpled, and she, too, burst into tears. She chewed her lips and nodded as she sobbed, releasing Wrath's and Bailey's hands to press her fingers to her mouth. "It's me, baby. I'm here. I've never stopped waiting for you. I knew I would see you again, I just knew it. I didn't know it would be like this," she said with a tearful chuckle. "But it's so good to hear your voice."

No matter how many times I'd seen it, hearing a voice that did not belong to the person using it was wild. I'd heard Jace Thornburgh use three different voices now. It was unsettling, but I couldn't deny the basic truth: the voice coming from him was not his own. Judging from Tamora's reaction, the speaker really was her husband, Jeff Bishop.

I'm telling you. Wonders never cease.

"There's so much I want to say to you," Jeff began.

"I hardly know where to start." Then he looked around the table, noticing for the first time that he and his wife were not alone. "Bailey? Vic? Heh." He smiled, meeting each woman's gaze with a chuckle. But then the smile slid from his face, and he asked, "Who are these other people?"

"Just friends," Tamora breathed, shaking off the question. "Just people here to help the two of us find each other."

Jeff balked. Everyone I'd spoken to mentioned how private Jeff was, and apparently, they were right. When he realized he had an audience, he clammed up. He shrank back into his chair, chin trembling. "I don't know about this, Tam-Tam. It doesn't feel right to talk to you with these strangers here. Can't we go anywhere private? Can't we—"

"The spell will break," Andromeda said, her voice tender but decisive. "I'm afraid none of us can leave the table, or we may lose you again."

He looked around, taking in the faces of the attendants. His gaze fell first to Bailey. "Hey, sis," he said, a crooked smile forming over his mouth. "How's tricks?"

Bailey grinned, a single tear falling down her cheek. "Hey, Jeff. It's good to talk to you again. Are you…are you well?"

I knew from experience how weird it was to talk to dead people. It's surprisingly awkward. You can't make small talk about the local sports team or what everyone's bingeing on Netflix. The weather is usually a safe topic unless the ghost is trapped indoors. But the point is, we're used to talking with people who are, you know, *living,* so we ask about *life.* Asking a dead guy how he's doing just seems like kicking a fellow when he's down.

"I'm hanging in there, all things considered," he said. He turned his gaze to Victoria, who looked like she'd swallowed a bug. "It's great to see you, Vic. I mean, really great. I have so much to say to you, too. But given our circumstances, I'll just say…I hope I made it up to you."

Victoria didn't move, but her mouth dropped open, and a tiny phrase emerged from her lips. "Thank you," was all she said.

A quick glance around the table told me that no one but Wrath and I understood the significance of the exchange. Even in death, Jeff still carried the guilt about his childhood with Victoria. Did he feel bad about the torture she endured at the hands of the poltergeists? Or was he sorry that his family dumped her when he went off to college, leaving her once again with nothing? It was impossible to say, and we might never know. But judging by the look on Victoria's face, none of that mattered.

She looked at peace.

At the other end of the table, Andromeda cleared her throat. "Jeff, I'm afraid our time might be running out. If there's something you'd like to say to Tamora, now is your chance."

Jeff shifted, rubbing his hands together as he peered at his wife. Her face was shining with tears, her chin wobbling. "I know we talked about getting married," Jeff said. "At the time, I thought it was a good idea. But that's because I accepted I might never cross back over.

If I'm going to be stuck here, I'd rather be stuck here with you. But truly, Tam-Tam, I'd rather not be stuck here. Being an intruder in another man's body…it's awful. Most of the time, I have no control. It's like being asleep, but it's not restful. I only wake up when Cecil is in charge of the body. And even then, I can only wake up when Cecil's guard is down, which isn't often. Every time I wake up, I try to escape and return to the other side. But it's like the other personalities I'm with hold me back. It feels like I'm tied down. Restrained. I'm a captive. That's the only way to say it."

Jeff was quiet a minute, his nostrils flaring, lips trembling. "Remember our first trip to Puerta Vallarta? You lost your purse and the key to our Airbnb. You waited for me on the porch, but I'd left a note on the bed saying I had a surprise for you. I was waiting for you at that Mediterranean restaurant. You never showed up because you never got the note. Remember?"

Tamora sniffled at the memory. "Yes, of course I remember. I waited for you for hours. I had no way to contact you because I'd lost my phone. After that, I memorized your phone number." She smiled softly, her eyes shining in the candlelight.

"That's right. That's how I feel now, Tam-Tam, except worse. Like I'm anxiously waiting for you. Seeing you lights me up inside, but the waiting—the times I'm asleep or trying to claw my way to the front—it's the worst. It hurts."

Tamora lowered her head, her voice tremulous. "Please, Jeff. Don't do this. If you leave Cecil's body, you'll really be dead. Again."

"Being dead's not so bad, really. It's a lot less stress-ful." He cracked a smile at his joke, but it slid quickly from his face. "If I have the choice, I don't want to spend the next however-many years trapped in someone else's body. Can you understand that?"

Tamora was openly crying again, her shoulders quaking with each sob. I saw Bailey squeeze her sister's fingers, offering what small comfort she could. When Tamora gathered herself enough to speak, she said, "I don't know if I can go on without you, Jeff. I already lost you once. It's not fair to ask me to lose you again."

Jeff sighed, nodding thoughtfully as he mulled over Tamora's words. "We're going to lose each other again, one way or another," Jeff said. "Either I will watch you die while trapped in someone else's body, or you lose me today or some unknown time in the future. And think about it this way, my love. What if I'm not even in control of this body when one of us passes? What happens then? At least doing it this way means we can say goodbye."

Tamora was really crying now. My heart ached for her. Death was supposed to be the period at the end of the sentence. It was supposed to close old doors while opening new ones. But this coming back and forth? Not only was it unnatural, it was unhealthy. Humans need closure. It's how we know it's time to breathe again.

"I just love you so much," Tamora was saying. "And I just can't imagine the rest of my life without you."

"I want you to find happiness," Jeff said. "I want you to find love again. Enjoy your sister's company. Enjoy the friendships you formed on your own." He said this last bit while gesturing around the table. "You have so much life left, and so much light to give, Tam-Tam. I won't take that from you. I want you to move on."

Tamora devolved into tears again and couldn't respond. While Tamora sobbed silently, Jeff nodded to Andromeda and settled back into his chair. "I'm ready," he said.

The medium lifted her hands to the ceiling. "I call upon the harmonies of the universe, the vibrations that move through all things. I call to the Great Beyond, to the Eternal Hereafter, to the Far Shore. Open your gates to our friend Jeff Bishop. Shine a beacon that can call him home. Show us the way, O Darkness! Show us the way, O Light! If you, Jeff Bishop, wish to be free of your current prison, come unite with me. I invite you into my body. I make room for you in my body. I will celebrate and release you in this body."

A rush of wind whistled through the room, and the candles stuttered out. The table shook, the legs screeching across the floor just as they had during the first séance. The tarot cards rose from the table, spinning and flipping this way and that as they floated in the air. Next, the collection of daggers clattered to the floor as the table shook more violently. With a lurch, the table jolted into the air, levitating ever higher. An earth-rumbling sound like an oncoming train thundered through the room. And then, seemingly from every-where at once, came Jeff Bishop's voice. "I accept your invitation, Andromeda. Bring me into your body so you can release me."

Jeff's voice was so loud, it rattled my bones. I felt like

he was inside my head, hollering his brains out. Everyone else must have been experiencing something similar because they were all looking around the room with hands pressed to their ears.

Jace/Cecil/Jeff was slack in his seat. He'd fallen sideways, eyes closed, chin dipped against his chest. At the other end of the table, Andromeda's hair had come loose and was floating about her shoulders. Her mouth dropped open and her head fell back, and in the darkness, I heard a voice booming from her body, "I'll never stop loving you, Tam-Tam."

And then it was over.

The table crashed to the floor. Candles fell and rolled, toppling to the ground. Someone screamed. Someone else was crying. At my side, Lust was hugging herself and whimpering. As for me, I'd seen all this before. Amazing how, if you've seen one séance, you've seen them all. I didn't care about the room's wishy-washy relationship with gravity.

I only cared whether Jeff was gone.

As the room stilled, Andromeda slowly woke up. She blinked and shook herself, dusting stray plastic spiders from her shoulders as she looked down the table. "Cecil?"

I turned my head to find our guest of honor struggling into wakefulness himself. He dug his knuckles into his eye sockets and rubbed. When he opened his eyes again, he said, "Is everyone okay?"

"We're fine," Andromeda breathed with a smile. "You're back. How do you feel?"

Cecil was quiet for a moment. Then he looked up

and nodded. "Like myself. Like a burden has been released." He smiled, but there was a note of sadness in it. I think that was for Tamora's benefit. He looked right at her when he said, "I think Jeff is in a good place. I feel joy where I used to feel his sorrow."

Andromeda leaned forward. "So, he's gone?"

Cecil smiled. "He's gone. You did it. He's…free."

For a minute, no one moved. But then Tamora drew slowly to her feet. She walked over to where Cecil sat, her face as expressionless as a mannequin's. And then, surprising everyone, she leaned down and enveloped him in a hug. "Thank you for keeping him safe as long as you did," she said. "And thank you for coming here and letting me say goodbye."

Cecil stood and hugged her back, and the two stayed that way for a long time.

# eighteen

### . . .

There's nothing quite like being at Sinful House after you've completed one task but haven't yet started another. I got to spend my days however I wanted. Cameras didn't follow me around as I walked along the beach, digging my toes in the sand and enjoying the ocean spray in my hair. Nobody peppered me with ridiculous questions when I walked down to the bakery and ordered a box full of scones and croissants. And importantly, I could waste time doing nothing without feeling guilty. No nagging worries over the poor schmuck whose crime I was supposed to be solving. The days after completing a task were truly awesome. When you weren't mired in local politics or weird paranormal activity, Odyssey was actually a nice place to be.

So I was thinking about how I wanted to spend the day when I found Lust sitting outside on the porch doing a puzzle on the ground. She looked up when she saw me, a grin breaking out over her face. Man, she looked so good when she smiled. Not that she didn't look good when she wasn't smiling. And believe me, I'm not the jerk that tells people they should smile more. But when she looks at me like that? It just makes me feel like I'm the only person on earth. And who doesn't love to feel that way?

But even though I felt that way, I wasn't gonna own up to it. I donned my best air of casual disinterest and asked, "What's this supposed to be?" I toed the edge of the puzzle with my shoe.

Lust leaned back into her hands. "Baby raccoons," she said. "I picked it up at Target yesterday. We solved our case, too, you know."

I nodded. "Yeah, I heard. Congratulations. You, Greed, and Envy tracked down some old guy's stolen antique guns, right?"

Lust nodded. "Yes. Well, mostly it was Greed. He figured it out after helping with your case. He realized old Mr. Sampson had something called 'intermittent dementia' and hid the guns from himself. Or something. Anyway, we found the guns in a safe deposit box at the bank." She sighed and blew a stray lock of hair from her eyes. "It sure wasn't as exciting as your case. But I'm glad we're both through with the grueling stuff. It's nice to just poke around and work on jigsaw puzzles. Or do…" She smiled at me. "…Whatever."

You know how sometimes an opportunity presents itself, and you feel like you have to grab it with both hands, or else you'll end up the world's biggest loser? But at the same time, your monkey brain is telling you that risk = possible failure. And if you fail:

1. You'll end up miserable and alone
2. No one will ever love you
3. Rambunctious neighborhood kids will throw rotten eggs at your house every morning,
4. And you'll never smile again.

You know that feeling?

That's how I felt at that moment.

*Ask her out*, my brain screamed at me. And I knew I should. I knew she liked me. She'd told me so a million times. Well, maybe not a million, but at least five, anyway. And if she said no, the *worst* that would happen is I'd feel embarrassed for a while, and then I'd get over it. I didn't even own a house, so I didn't need to worry about rambunctious neighborhood kids.

But...I didn't want to be embarrassed. We lived together. I'd have to see her every day. And what if she told someone I'd asked her out, and they giggled about it like it was the funniest thing in the world? Because yeah, she was out of my league. Totally. But still...?

I must've stood there debating what to say for too long because Lust laughed and cut her eyes at me, her head cocked to the side. "Cat got your tongue, Freak Show? Come on, Pride. I know you. What's eating you?"

I quirked an eyebrow. "Eating me? Oh." I dug my hands in my pockets. "That's a metaphor."

She nodded. "Yes. What's *bothering* you?"

I sucked in a breath and closed my eyes. *Here goes nothing*, I thought. "The other day at the citywide garage sale, I wasn't the shopping partner you deserved. I want to make up for that."

Lust sucked her teeth. "You bought me a tiara. Consider that score settled."

"No, that's not what I mean." I opened my eyes and stared down at my feet. Why was I such a moron with words? I didn't want to be her shopping buddy! This wasn't about making things up to her! Why was it so hard to say what I really meant?

"It's just that I was wondering, if you're not busy, did you want to… I don't know. Spend the day with me?"

A sly smile spread over Lust's face. "My goodness, Pride. Are you asking me on a date?"

My face flushed so hot, I thought I might spontaneously combust. "Yes," I said.

Lust sat forward and brushed her hands together. "I accept," she said, climbing to her feet. She linked her arm in mine and led me back into the house. "What did you have in mind?"

I didn't have anything in mind. Literally nothing. As soon as Lust accepted my invitation, all other thoughts evaporated from my brain. I was a walking ball of goo with an IQ of -500 and the only thing running through my brain was *she said yes she said yes* repeatedly.

But finally, thankfully, I pulled myself together enough to ask, "What sounds good to you?"

"There's an art gallery I'd like to check out," she said. "You don't really strike me as an artsy person, but—"

"I love art," I blurted. That was a lie. I didn't know a thing about art except that a child could do it, and some art looked like a child *did* do it. But if it made me look better in Lust's eyes, I could love anything. Almost anything. I would never love shopping. "I'm a huge art fan. Did you want to go now?"

Lust chuckled. "Can I have, say, 20 minutes? I need to put my face on." She paused, then added, "I mean, I have to put on some makeup."

"Got it," I said. "I'll meet you back here in 20."

While Lust piled her face with products she didn't need, I scuttled back to my room to change into something more date-worthy. I shuffled through my closet, immediately rejecting every piece of clothing I owned. Grateful Dead t-shirt? Too casual. Pressed white button-down? Too formal. Cozy cashmere sweater? Way too warm. I rejected my favorite plaid pullover, my vintage Care Bear t-shirts, and my trusty knit jacket. Nothing was good enough, but so help me, I was *not* going to ask Envy for help, not after the last time she'd dressed me like a color-blind clown.

I was looking under my bed, hoping that's where the miraculous perfect outfit might be hiding, when a voice behind me said, "She's not gonna care what you wear, you know. Since when do you care about appearances?"

"Since always," I answered. "Everyone cares about appearances. Anyone who says otherwise is selling something."

"That's not true," the ghost girl retorted. "And anyway, haven't you been through everything you own? Why isn't what you've got on okay?"

"It's gonna have to be," I grumbled, resigned to the reality that a trip to a shopping mall was in my future. I needed to invest in something better than a t-shirt but not as lame as a button-down.

"Where are you guys going? The museum? Ice skating? The dog park?"

"Neither one of us has a dog," I pointed out. "Why would we go to the dog park?"

The ghost ignored this. "Did you know dogs can have a sense of smell that's like one hundred times better than ours?"

"That sounds high to me," I grumbled. I was rifling through my sock drawer, looking for the twin to the Yoda trouser sock I held in one hand. "Maybe it's only like 10 times as good."

I could see the sock now. It was wedged in the back of the drawer. I wriggled the drawer in its tracks, trying to get the sock loose, but it was really jammed in there.

"No, it's like one hundred. Maybe even *two* hundred," the ghost girl insisted.

I didn't feel like arguing with her. It's fine if ghosts get their facts wrong. It's not like they're going to spread misinformation on social media and stir up trouble. And even if she did, what harm could it do to let people think dogs had supernatural powers of smell?

I tried to yank the drawer free, but it wasn't coming out. I jiggled and tugged, cursing the manufacturer. "You gotta be kidding me," I whined. Then I yanked the stupid drawer as hard as I could.

The drawer finally jerked free, but the force of my pulling shook the dresser so hard that the things I'd tossed up there fell and slid off. The lamp fell onto its side and rolled to the floor. But before it fell, it crashed into Walt's laptop. Both lamp and laptop smashed to the floor.

"Oh no," I moaned, dropping the drawer.

"I thought you were taking that to the police," the ghost said.

"I was supposed to," I agreed. "I just didn't make the time."

The laptop screen was cracked, and the plastic casing that attached the screen to the lid had come loose. I bent down to pick up the now-busted machine and noticed something strange.

I crouched over the laptop. The corner of a piece of paper was sticking out from behind the screen. Gingerly, I pulled the paper free and spread it across my knees.

"What the…? Is this what I think it is?"

The ghost girl was hovering over my shoulder, peering down at the recovered paper. "Looks like some kind of map," she whispered.

Intersecting horizontal and vertical lines were obviously streets, but none were marked. Squares with triangles on top were buildings—maybe houses or perhaps businesses, but again, none were labeled. Some squares were bigger than others, but I couldn't tell if that was because the map had been sketched quickly or if the difference in scale was intentional. There was no key. A collection of half ovals looked like they might be graves, but I couldn't be sure. The ovals were marked with a star, and scribbled across the bottom were the words, "Historic Odyssey Nexus of Power, 1902."

I sucked in a breath as realization struck me. *This* was the hidden information the laptop concealed. It wasn't a digital file at all, which was why Wrath couldn't find it. It was this piece of paper—this shoddily drawn, indecipherable, sorry excuse for a map.

"Somebody went to a lot of trouble to hide that," the ghost said, still whispering. "You should probably keep that safe. Put it somewhere good."

I left the broken laptop where it was and scanned my room. "Yeah, you're right. Whoever killed Mrs. Romanowsky likely killed her for this map," I said, more to myself than the ghost. "But I don't know where to put it. I wonder if I—"

My door opened, and Lust poked her head inside. As a house, we really needed to get better at respecting other people's privacy. "You ready?"

"Just one second," I said, hiding the paper behind my back. "Meet you downstairs in two?"

Lust pulled the door closed, and I carefully lodged the map between my mattress and box spring. It was a terrible hiding place and probably the first place a killer would look. But I'd have to find a more suitable place later when I wasn't in such a rush.

"Do me a favor," I said to the ghost. "Don't let anyone in my room until I come home."

The ghost rolled her eyes, her hands splayed out before her. "And how am I supposed to do that? I can't even touch anybody!"

I tossed her a wink and pulled my Yoda socks onto my feet. "You'll think of something," I said.

Then I rushed down the stairs, heart skipping into my throat as I headed to my first date with Lust.

The Odyssey Museum of Modern Art was a beautiful glass building by the sea. As Lust and I entered, her arm linked in mine and my hands dug into my pockets, I marveled that such a building could exist shoulder to shoulder with the strange things I'd seen in this town. How could something as mundane as a modern art museum exist in a city where ghosts had their own secret society and old ladies got murdered by supernatural bounty hunters?

Still, as we walked into the building, feeling the crisp, conditioned air riffle our hair, tension dripped from my shoulders. Even the cameramen tagging along weren't stressing me out for once. (I'd tried to escape without them, but they were insistent. "It's a great human-interest angle!" my camera guy asserted, jamming a peanut butter sandwich into his mouth. "Network would kill me if I let you lovebirds on a date alone.") I was content to be in an ordinary place doing everyday things.

Not that being on a date with a beautiful woman was normal for me. In fact, my hands were in my pockets to stop myself from pinching my arms to make sure I wasn't dreaming.

Ahead, a group of schoolchildren on a field trip ran from exhibit to exhibit, loudly and excitedly admiring the paintings and sculptures on display. Lust pressed her body against mine, smiling in excitement. "Where should we start?" She was craning her neck, her head swiveling from side to side as she scanned our options.

"Do you want to browse on your own, or should we ask someone for a guided tour?"

Both options sounded terrifying. Being alone with Lust was what I wanted in theory, but then the burden of entertaining her would fall to me alone. On the other hand, a guided tour might be helpful, except I didn't want some rando tagging along.

However, the decision was wrenched from my hands when a young docent approached us, smiling with an enthusiasm usually reserved for toddlers and Golden Retrievers. He was college-age with rosy cheeks and a tan that indicated he might be a local. He was dressed in a crisp navy-blue blazer and tan chinos. "Welcome to OMMA," he said. "Have the two of you been here before?"

Lust shook her head. "First time!" she exclaimed. "Do you have any pointers?"

The docent clapped his hands together and faced Lust squarely, ignoring me. "Of course! We have several tracks to help our patrons enjoy all we offer. The exhibit starts on the bottom floor and winds its way up to the second, third, and fourth floors. If you want to see everything in the museum, expect to spend five hours on the premises. There's a lovely cafeteria on the second floor if you need to take a break. However, if your time is limited, we have story tracks that guide you on a more curated tour. You can choose from our tracks dedicated to local artists, female artists, artists with disabilities, or artists of color. Or, if a thematic tour is preferred, we have tours for mind-bending experiences, Americana, slice of life, and abstract appreciation. Or, if none of these options appeals to you, I can take you on a personalized tour highlighting some of my favorite pieces."

Lust turned to me, her face expectant. "It all sounds fantastic," she gushed. "What would you like to do?"

What I wanted to do was not make this decision. But it looked like I had to choose something, so I said, "A guided tour sounds great."

The young man took a step forward and pressed his palm against his chest. "Well, in that case, my name is Greg, and I will gladly be your docent for the day. And you are?"

"Pride," I said.

"And I'm Lust."

He was definitely a local (or maybe he'd just seen the show) because he wasn't at all surprised by our introductions. He extended a hand, which we both shook. "Well, it's a pleasure to have you at the museum. If neither of you has questions, why don't we get started?"

As it turned out, exploring the museum wasn't as arduous an experience as I feared. I usually associated modern art with splatter paintings or giant squares of a single color—neither of which I understood. But these paintings had soul. There were paintings of women screaming as they watched their children play at recess. A huge portrait showed a man crying in his corner office. Other images depicted animals, ocean landscapes, and, of course, they had obligatory abstract art. Interspersed with the paintings were sculptures. I liked the fiber art best. Some enterprising artist named Annabella Schwartz created a life-size pride of lions out of felt and yarn. It was an impressive display.

"I wanted to be an artist when I was young," Lust told the docent as we meandered up the stairs. "My parents couldn't be bothered with it, though. Sometimes I wonder about the artists who get to show at galleries. Did their parents support them from the beginning, or did they learn to fly on their own?"

"It's an interesting question," the docent said with a nod. "Everyone's story is different. We have a painting by a man named Pedro Fernandez who didn't start painting until he was 75."

The docent led us to the far corner of the second floor. "Over here is a personal favorite. This simple painting of a fisher catching a bass truly captures the zeitgeist and the profound loneliness and disappointment that most of us experience in our everyday lives."

I examined the painting. An angler adrift in an empty lake was reeling a large bass from the water. The line had snapped, and the bass was falling to the lake as the fisherman watched in bewilderment. Whether it captured the zeitgeist of loneliness or whatever was up for debate, but it was a nice painting.

Lust read the title of the piece from a placard on the wall. "*A Quiet Fisherman Drops the Bass*," she said.

The docent's eyebrows shot up. "*A Quiet Fisherman Drops the* Bass," he said, correcting her pronunciation. She'd read "bass" like in music, rhyming with "base." He read it with a short a, rhyming with "pass."

Lust chuckled. "Well, it's sort of a double entendre, isn't it?" she asked.

The docent frowned, puzzled. "How do you mean?"

Lust shrugged and gestured at the title with a flick of

her wrist. "Well, because of the word *bass*. It's obviously a picture of a fisherman, so you might read it as bass like the fish. But it's also a dubstep thing. When the bassline thumps hard, you know? They dropped the bass. So you could call this painting *A Quiet Fisherman Drops the Bass*" (She said it with short a, like the fish), "or you could read it *A Quiet Fisherman Drops the Bass*" (This time, she used a long a, like the instrument). "They're spelled the same way on paper but pronounced differently aloud."

The docent peered at her as though she had a second head growing out of her neck. "I assure you, the painting is titled *A Quiet Fisherman Drops the Bass*," he said, pronouncing bass like the fish.

She held up her hands defensively. "I'm not arguing. That could be how it's pronounced. But it could go the other way, too. I'm just saying it's a pretty clever joke."

"But it's not music," the docent insisted, his face pinched. His eyes flit briefly to me and then back to Lust. "It's a *painting*. It's *art*. It's not a record album."

Both Lust and Greg-the-docent had a point, and I wasn't sure who won the argument. But just as I was preparing to interrupt (their argument was going nowhere and I was getting annoyed), I noticed the complete title of the piece on the wall. The placard said, "*A Quiet Fisherman Drops the Bass* on canvas."

The words "on canvas" caught my attention, and I paused, my hand going to my mouth as my mind reeled.

Instantly, I was transported back to the séance where Andromeda spoke in that strange voice and said to me, "Some of all profits on vinyl."

Andromeda thought it was the name of an album. But now, I wondered. Maybe it wasn't the name of an album at all. What if "on vinyl" just meant vinyl was the surface medium?

What if the voice coming from Andromeda's body was referring not to an album but a piece of art?

"Greg," I said suddenly, "are you familiar with the story of the Sam Lovelace commune that disappeared all those years ago?"

"Oh, yes!" Now that he was back on solid ground, the docent's thousand-watt smile returned. "I wrote my master's thesis on the commune's aims. Art that heals," he intoned, making a rainbow gesture with his hands. "Really a noble idea. Too bad they all vanished. Why do you ask?"

"Have you heard of an art piece that might have come from there called *Some of All Profits?*"

The docent twisted his mouth in thought. "I'm not sure," he said. "It sounds familiar, but..." He dug a phone from his pocket and clicked around. Then he snapped his fingers in the air with a nod. "Aha! Yes, here it is. It's owned by a private collector in Santa Barbara. Is this the piece you mean?"

He showed me the phone. A dozen records were glued together as a canvas onto which the artist had painted a troubling scene. A group of people with no faces were being attacked by a mob of unruly spirits while a robed wise man in the corner counted out his money without helping the others.

The piece was titled, *Sum of All Prophets* on vinyl.

I stared, my mouth agape. Another play on words,

just like *Drop the Bass*. Not *Some of All Profits*, but *Sum of All Prophets*. That's why I never found a reference to it the night I'd googled the phrase with the ghost girl. I'd been using the wrong words.

"Lust," I whispered, "that's it. *That's* the clue I'm meant to find."

"Clue?" The docent tucked the phone back into his pocket. "Can I be a complete buttinsky and ask—a clue about what?"

"About my past," I said, my head still spinning. "I was the baby rescued from the compound. And I think that artwork was created by…"

Lust blinked, her eyes wide. "By *who*, Pride?"

I swallowed hard, remembering the eerily familiar voice that drifted from Andromeda's body that night. I knew now why some primitive part of me had recognized it. Some things are so sacred, they become imprinted on your brain. Or your soul. Or something.

I swallowed in a dry throat. "I think that artwork was created by my mother."

I glanced back at the camera crew. Man, the network was gonna have a field day with this.

# nineteen

. . .

few nights later, it was time for the mortifying task of watching ourselves on TV while we awaited the arrival of producer Tricia. Gluttony had set out trays full of hors d'oeuvres, and Lust was passing around a bottle of champagne. We were all watching the last episode of our first task. I have to say, it's weird to watch your life unfold weeks after you've already lived it. I mean, I get it. The network had to delay our episodes—it would be impossible to air the show in real time. Still, we were about to start our third task, and America had just seen the conclusion of our first.

I was sitting next to Sloth, both of us stuffing our faces with popcorn, when Tricia breezed through the front door. "Hi everyone! How's it going? Did everyone watch tonight's episode?"

I looked over my shoulder and waved. "Hi, Tricia," I said. "Yes, we watched. It was awful."

Tricia looked around the room. "Any problems with *editing* this time?" She directed this question at Wrath.

The surly technopath was still watching the TV, a scowl on his face and arms crossed over his chest. "I still think they didn't give me a fair shot, man," he grumbled. "But at least I looked good in most of the episodes. Americans are shallow. They like anything that looks good. Which is a problem because unrealistic beauty standards established by Big Media reward—"

"Thanks, Wrath, I'll take your feedback to the rest of the team," Tricia interrupted. "I have the updates on your scores, everyone! Before I read these, please keep in mind that this is just the beginning of the season. You still have plenty of time to win over the viewers. So, if you didn't perform well this week, just remember, it's still early."

Tricia whipped out her phone and began reading. "In seventh place with 8% of the vote is Sloth. Greed, you came in sixth place with 10% of the vote. Gluttony, you're in fifth place with 11%. Envy, you got 12% and are in fourth place this week. In third place is Pride, with 14% of the vote. Lust, you're in second with a whopping 20%. And this week's winner, with a very improbable 25% of the vote, is—inexplicably—Wrath."

Cheers and jeers went up from my housemates. Everyone was laughing and pointing at Wrath, whose eyes were wide and round, his mouth open. Even he couldn't believe that he'd actually won this week.

"Well, bad editing aside, looks like you're doing pretty well for yourself, Wrath," Tricia joked, eyebrow cocked. "Got anything to say? Any vitriol to spew about your fellow Americans?"

Wrath shook his head and jammed his hands into

the kangaroo pocket of his hoodie. "Well, you know what they say. People often make up in wrath what they lack in reason," he said with a sly grin.

"That's…not a positive for you," Envy pointed out.

"Maybe not, but I got the votes, and you can take that to the bank."

"But banks are the foundation of capitalism, Wrath! I thought you—"

"All right," Tricia interrupted again, smiling. "Are you all ready for your next assignments?" She didn't wait for an answer. With her face tipped toward her phone, she began reading. "For this week's task, the teams will be as follows. Wrath, since you are this week's winner, you'll be paired with Sloth. Pride, you will work with Envy. The last group will comprise Lust, Gluttony, and Greed."

"Together again," Greed said, making eyes at Lust. "Maybe this time, we'll bring home the win."

"I sure hope so," she purred, sidling up beside him and linking her arm in his. "I'm tired of playing second fiddle to these jokers."

I pretended not to watch them, but seeing Lust snuggling up next to Greed made me faint with nausea. What was she doing? And why right here in front of everyone? Okay, true, we weren't a couple or anything. But I thought we had something going.

But now, watching her make goo-goo eyes at Greed, I wasn't so sure.

Envy drew up beside me, nodding her head toward Lust and Greed. "I bet that makes you want to jam your thumb in your eye, huh?" she said, her mouth twisted in a frown. "I'm jealous on your behalf just watching them. I mean, seriously, get a room, you know? Have some shame, for goodness' sake."

I swallowed and turned my back to the confusing scene, trying to keep my expression light. "Don't worry about me," I said. "Lust can do what she likes. I don't own her, you know?"

"No, of course not. But it just doesn't seem fair. You bought her that tiara, you took her to the art gallery, you—"

"Envy, stop. It's fine." It wasn't. "I'm okay." I wasn't. "She's…I mean, that's who she is, right? She's Lust. A tiger can't change its stripes."

Envy scowled. "I guess. But—"

"No, I should have known better," I said, my throat dry. "You fall for a girl like that, and you're bound to get your heart stomped on. Listen, I'll be right back. I need to talk to Tricia before she leaves."

Tricia was already gathering her things and headed to the front door. I put a hand on her shoulder, and she turned. "Pride," she said. "What is it? Everything okay?"

*Everything is* not *okay*, I thought desperately. *I thought I met someone, I thought maybe someone was falling for me, and now I realize I'm just a name in her little black book. Why, WHY am I such a moron?!*

But instead of saying any of that, I swallowed down my panic. "I want to talk to you about my upcoming assignment with Envy."

Tricia's eyebrows shot up. "Oh? Did you have a question about it? I thought it was straightforward."

I shook my head. "No, we haven't even read it yet.

Uh, I was wondering. I've been doing what the network wanted me to do. Looking into the Sam Lovelace thing."

Tricia nodded. "I've seen some of the footage from the séance," she said. "It's good stuff."

"Yeah, well, I have a request. Some new information came to light recently. It looks like I might have to take a trip up to Santa Barbara."

Tricia smiled. "Santa Barbara is gorgeous this time of year. Every time of year, really. Are you going up to the site? The place where the commune was before it vanished?"

"No," I said, though that was actually not a bad idea. "There's something I need to see. A piece of art. When Andromeda channeled that spirit that first night at Tamora's, it spoke to me, remember? It said, *"Find Sum of All Prophets.* Well, turns out that's an art piece owned by a private collector up in Santa Barbara. I've arranged to meet with him already."

Tricia stepped closer to me, her eyes twinkling. I could almost hear the *cha-ching!* of a cash register dinging in her mind. "That's *excellent* news, Pride! The network will be so happy to hear that!"

"Yeah, well, there's a snag, though. Santa Barbara's a good five hours from here. That's not a quick back-and-forth trip."

"It could be," Tricia said with a shrug. "I've done worse."

"Okay, but the point is, I'll need time while I'm up there. You know, to do some proper investigative work. Which means I might not have a lot of time left to work on whatever the network assigned me. So I'm just wondering…Maybe Envy and I can work on the missing commune case and skip whatever cockamamie mystery you put us on for this task?"

Tricia chuckled with a rueful shake of her head. "You know that isn't how this works," she said. "Everybody has to do their fair share. But don't worry so much. I think you'll like the task you and Envy got. Still, I encourage you to go to Santa Barbara. Take all the time you need. You might not win your challenge, that's true. But the viewer votes you'll get for following a lead in the missing commune case? It'll be well worth it. Our audience will eat that *up*."

"That's not all," I continued. I checked over my shoulder to make sure no one was listening and that the cameras weren't trained on me. "I found something about Mrs. Romanowsky's murder."

Tricia narrowed her eyes. "I thought you decided to leave well enough alone. You said it was dangerous—and for the record, I agree. We never intentionally signed you up for harm," she said.

"I know. But I changed my mind. Now that I have a real lead, I can't let it go. I have to follow up on it."

Tricia weighed these words for a minute. Then she smoothed her hair behind her ears and cleared her throat. "That's up to you and Sloth, of course. You're both grown adults, and I can't stop you, not even if you're being foolish. But your task is your task."

"Tricia, I just think—"

"Well, don't," she said, patting me on the cheek.

"You don't need to think. The network did all the thinking for all seven of you. See you soon."

She left me standing there with my mouth hanging open as she breezed out the door.

Frustrated, I wandered back into the living room to find Envy curled up on the couch, gazing into her phone. When she saw me, she waved me over and patted the seat next to her. "You ready to see what our case is?"

I shrugged. At this point, I couldn't care less. I was already investigating a missing commune and a woman's murder related to supernatural bounty hunters. Whatever dumb assignment the network had dug up for us couldn't possibly hold a candle to *that*.

But I didn't say any of that, of course. "Do us the honors."

Envy clicked on an email titled, "Envy and Pride: Challenge #3."

The email read,

"The temporary residents of Remembrance Home have been experiencing strange moments of clarity. The proprietors of the establishment would like help discovering the cause of this strange awakening."

Envy looked up at me and shrugged. "That doesn't seem so bad."

At the end of the email was a link that just said, "The details." Envy clicked it.

A screen loaded up. It said,

"Remembrance Home is a mortuary, and the embalmed corpses awaiting their final viewing have begun to talk. It's your job to find out how and why."

I looked at Envy and snorted, halfway because her expression was so funny and halfway because—well. That thing I just said about how my next task couldn't possibly be that interesting?

I guess I was wrong.

# thanks for reading!

*Sinful House Mysteries* was so much fun to write, and I'm thrilled to share these adventures with you.

I'd love it if we kept in touch.

If you'd like that too, please sign up for my newsletter on my website.

If a newsletter isn't your jam but you'd still like to support me, please consider leaving a review. This is the easiest and best way to help other readers connect with the weird and wonderful cast at *Sinful House*.

See you soon!

# about the author

Amber Fisher is the author of urban fantasy and paranormal mysteries ranging from sweet and delightful to dark and morbid. She lives in Austin, Texas, where she enjoys watching sci-fi shows, making things with her hands, baking, and playing tabletop games with her husband.

Connect with me at: amberfishermedia.com

Facebook at: facebook.com/amberfisherauthor

Twitter: @amberla

Sign up for the newsletter: bit.ly/332eurl